Conflict—

"Robyn, where've you been till this hour?"

"I had to keep an appointment, in town."

"I know that you've been with your father." Her mother's voice was shrill, menacing.

"You're shouting, Mother."

"Don't you criticize me! Your father's dead! He is to me! He should be to you!"

"Now you listen to me," Robyn said, struggling to remain calm. "My father, Robert Adam, came out of prison today. He is now on parole, after being shut away for six years."

"You mean, *Robert's been dead* for six years!"

"Not to me, Mom! And you can't forbid me to see him. That's what you're getting ready to do, aren't you?"

"Yes!"

"Well, don't!"

"Robyn, why are you doing this to us. . . .?"

Robyn didn't know how she could explain it to her mother. Yet somehow she had to make her understand, before it was too late, that knowing and helping her father had become the most important thing in her life. . . .

ADAM'S DAUGHTER

SIGNET Fiction You'll Enjoy

ADAM'S DAUGHTER

Gertrude Samuels

A SIGNET BOOK

NEW AMERICAN LIBRARY

TIMES MIRROR

This is an authorized reprint of a hardcover edition published by
Thomas Y. Crowell Company, Inc. The hardcover edition was
published simultaneously in Canada by
Fitzhenry & Whiteside Limited, Toronto.

Ⓢ

SIGNET TRADEMARK REG. U.S. PAT. OFF. AND FOREIGN COUNTRIES
REGISTERED TRADEMARK—MARCA REGISTRADA
HECHO EN CHICAGO, U.S.A.

SIGNET, SIGNET CLASSICS, MENTOR, PLUME AND MERIDIAN BOOKS
are published by The New American Library, Inc.,
1301 Avenue of the Americas, New York, New York 10019

First Signet Printing, January, 1979

3   4   5   6   7   8   9   10   11

PRINTED IN THE UNITED STATES OF AMERICA

For Bernard,
in grateful and loving memory

Author's Note

All the names of persons in this book are fictional, and any resemblance to actual persons, living or dead, is entirely coincidental.

In gathering material for this documentary novel, I was fortunate to have the close cooperation of many local and national experts in the law, psychology, prison conditions and parole, and of ex-offenders themselves, in my travels across the country, from New York to California. My deep thanks go to all of them in this endeavor.

The story of *Adam's Daughter* is taken from true episodes—from life itself.

—*G. S.*

Two roads diverged in a wood, and I—
I took the one less traveled by,
And that has made all the difference.

from "The Road Not Taken"
by Robert Frost

1.

The early evening that twentieth of March was like any other inside the Port Authority Bus Terminal in Manhattan. It was the city's rush hour, and the scene was one of total frenzy. It assaulted the girl's senses as she entered, trying to nerve herself for what she must soon cope with. She stood aside, steadying herself, watching . . .

Streams of people with parcels and suitcases struggling frantically to reach their ticket lines. Others elbowing one another at the newsstand for the evening paper or magazines for the homebound trips. Others hurrying into shops for last-minute purchases. Scores rushing to the escalators which, momentarily, bound people together. Hardhats from some construction site shoving past a crowd of commuters. Dark-suited business types with chromium-etched brief cases, disappearing into the Post & Coach Inn for "a quick one for the road." Servicemen with duffel bags, bunched together, hurrying . . .

And everywhere children—children hanging on to their parents, twisting away from parents, being hauled back, one or two getting a slap for their trouble.

She tried to shake off her confusion and fears, and slowly moved into the human parade. She had time. Time to note the policemen, standing deliberately on view on the rim of the crowds, or walking inside them, their billies and holstered guns showing prominently on their wide leather belts, cowboy fashion. And why not? she thought, rebuking herself. The terminal was a well-known tourist trap, a rich human vein mined by the underworld, by muggers and pickpockets, pimps and prostitutes. I'm being too sensitive!

The crowds milled around her, shoving at her indifferently, or trying to avoid her as she moved too slowly for them. Now she stared at the huge clock. It hung, abstract and inexorable, twenty feet above the people, its black hands warning all of them. Her mind fastened on the clock, helping to shut out the forest of strange faces. What had he asked her? Not to go to the arrival gate to meet him—"There may be others coming out with me," he had said haltingly, "and I think . . . I prefer to meet you under the clock, about six o'clock. Alone?"

Well, of course, alone. Who would come with her anyway? Who would want to? The clock told her she was twenty minutes ahead of time. She hurt with the excitement and uncertainty, suddenly wondering what *his* feelings must be on this last leg of his journey back to the outside world.

You might have come with me, Mom, she thought.

But that's impossible, isn't it?

That's why I couldn't tell you I was coming to meet him. But someone had to!

Someone . . . me.

I had to, didn't I?

Well, *didn't I?*

She stood motionless under the clock, too early for his arrival, assailed by her confused feelings as she stared up at the minute hand. A policeman walked near, swinging his billy. Incredibly she found herself shaking as though with guilt as the cop looked her over routinely. He walked on and joined his partner. You're being so stupid, she scolded herself; but the last thing she wanted was a cop's attention. So after a moment, she walked off, too, and went to the women's room.

The place was full of girls her own age, outfitted in camping clothes and canvas backpacks, and they were laughing and chattering about some bus trip they were about to take into the mountains. She could remember such a trip that *they'd* gone on . . . so many years ago.

The girls radiated such joyous expectation that it lifted her own spirits, briefly. The room seemed to be grotesquely silent after they left.

Her head was hurting. She ran some cold water over a paper towel and put it against her forehead and then her neck. Trying to ease the pain, but also some other inner burden that she could not quite put her finger on: Resentment at having been drawn into this episode? Guilt at having to deceive her mother? What was she doing here anyway? Was this *really* her responsibility—getting involved with someone who'd been . . . been in prison? She shook her head angrily, trying to put down the old torturous thoughts that could impugn her motives.

"You can stop the self-analysis. That's depraved," she told herself. "You're here now. One thing at a time, that's what you've promised yourself . . . and him."

She stared at herself in the wall mirror, and, almost mechanically, she began to brush her long, thick, auburn hair which hung loose to her shoulders. Brushing with hard strokes had become a ritual with her. She liked to think it helped to brush away her mental cobwebs, and, at this moment, the nagging, negative questions tormenting her. She savored the regular strokes against her pain, watching how her hair framed anew the high forehead, the large, dark brown eyes now brooding in the oval face.

"Cheer up, you!" she told the mirror-image, as she put the brush away, and began to adjust her large-loop, gold earrings. "Just be glad you didn't have your ears pierced for these two. You've got enough holes in your head!"

She giggled then, thankful that she could laugh at herself. Thankful, too, as she started back to the clock, that she was wearing her old blue jeans and denim jacket instead of the lovely yellow skirt and light sweater that Mom had bought her for her birthday. That fragile outfit wouldn't have a chance in this mob, she thought. Then, suddenly, she saw him standing under the clock.

Even inside that crazy, milling crowd, he looked terribly alone.

Tall, gaunt, his dark hair wispy and untidy above the

faded blue eyes and thin, beaky nose, he was scanning the people and seemed rigid with anxiety. Then he saw her coming, and his eyes shone with relief. He grabbed her to him, kissed her, and held her close.

"Hi, Daddy, how are you?"

"Ah, Robyn, you came!"

"Well, of course! What did you expect?"

"I don't know . . . I don't know!"

"Let's get away from this madhouse, Daddy. Have coffee, and talk."

"No, Robyn, uh, not just yet." He seemed suddenly vague, and she saw his face cloud. "I mean, not right away."

He was looking around in a lost sort of way, as though becoming aware of the crowds for the first time. She saw his look take in the cops. He flinched, pressing her hand hard, muttering, "There's something I have to do before we can sit and talk, Robyn. Okay?"

She nodded and took his arm. They had to walk past the cops, heading toward the Eighth Avenue exit, and after a moment he went on in a bitter monotone. "Don't be worried, Robyn girl. It's just . . . well, the cops can spot ex-cons a mile away. It's true," he said, reacting to her amazed look. "Oh, not by our faces, though they sure know what prison pallor is. Not our clothes or the bag. It's our *shoes,* believe it or not. Brand-new shiny shoes, Robyn, never been worn before, and that's what they look for!"

His bitter, clipped words fell on Robyn like a shower of stones. Cops . . . ex-cons . . . ex-convicts . . . shoes . . . shiny shoes . . . She stared ahead, feeling the pain knot her stomach, leading him deftly now around the people to the red exit light, on to the Avenue.

"What is it you must do first, Daddy?"

His face twisted with embarrassment. "Check in with my parole officer. The Department of Correction offices are just around the corner, they said, on Fortieth Street. They make it easy for us to check in, you know . . . offices close to the terminal," he said in a cynical tone. "So mustn't disobey."

But out on Eighth Avenue he seemed momentarily to lose his toughness, to panic before the aggressive street life. The evening traffic was dense, bumper to bumper, horns crying evil, people hurrying indifferent to everything, but carrying with them their own sense of uneasiness. Robyn saw her father back off in a kind of shock, pressing himself against the glass window of a Fanny Farmer Candy Shop. She took his hand, as though he were the child.

"It's just the rush hour. It's always this way."

"I guess so. I'd forgotten. It's been over six years, you know."

More than that, she thought.

A lifetime.

The pimps were out in force, walking in single file and in twos, black men and white, very sharp dressers from their broad-brimmed hats, colored shirts, and wide ties down to their platform soles. Their girls, with navels showing between their skimpy blouses and brief skirts, swung ahead of them, each pausing to approach some man or the window shoppers. One bosomy redhead began to approach her father, but then she saw Robyn, gave a sniff and kept moving. Robyn saw his face redden, but he stared after the woman. Then he twisted around, as though away from some painful memory, and began to study the brightly lit shop window. It featured boxes of "Fancy Pastels," "Pyramid Chocolates," and, tantalizingly, "Sulta Nut Meats—Try A Box Today."

And for the first time, Robyn heard him laugh. It came from deep within him, warm and cathartic and infectious. His old Dublin laugh, Mom had liked to call it once. "How about that, Robyn? A box of Sulta Nut Meats . . . *today?*"

"You've got to save your money, Daddy."

"But I didn't buy you anything for your birthday."

"That doesn't matter."

"Of course it matters! You're seventeen now . . . it

matters! Why, you're all grown up, aren't you? And very pretty, too. Shouldn't have to be worrying . . ." He broke off, and she saw the faded eyes mist over. "It matters." Then he laughed again. "It's got to be the whole box, Robyn girl, since I can't give you a *diamond!*"

She let him buy it for her then, partly because his laughter had been good to hear again, so Irish and spontaneous; partly because she knew that the father she had once adored, and for whom she was named, was remembering a favorite poem:

> *Little girl, little girl,*
> *Where have you been?*
> *Gathering roses*
> *To give to the Queen.*

> *Little girl, little girl,*
> *What gave she you?*
> *She gave me a diamond,*
> *As big as my shoe.*

He told the clerk to put a fancy wrapping on the box, and birthday ribbons. Then they walked west on Fortieth Street, past the liquor store and the Greek-American "Grocery & Deli" and "Duffy's Tavern" and a parking lot to her father's destination—a five-story, red-brick building with a large sign at the entrance:

> New York State
> Department of Correctional
> Services

The street was, like so many streets of New York's inner city, dreary and garbage littered. And the people walking or loitering there looked forgotten. A couple of derelicts were standing near the State building, drinking quite openly from their pint bottles. Robyn saw her father stare at them with a mixture of disbelief at their insolence and of fear. Was he remembering, then . . . ?

"You sure you want to come in?" he said. "I could meet you later, at the Center."

"You're stuck with me, Daddy," she said lightly, trying to hide her tension.

"Well, okay, I don't think this will take long."

"Don't forget to tell him—the parole officer—that you've been promised a nice studio apartment on the upper West Side, and I've put down the deposit. Tell him . . ."

"Tell him *nothing*!" he burst out in a rough tone. "It's just that," he went on hurriedly as he saw her flinch, "you learn inside prison to listen to everything and volunteer nothing. You just have to agree, to everything. Otherwise the P.O. can break you in five minutes if you 'fall.' "

" 'Fall'?"

"Oppose him and his instructions in any way. Violate parole."

"But the way I heard it, the P.O.'s are supposed to *help* a person," she protested.

"Some do."

"Some? Maybe you'll get lucky."

"Don't count on that. Robyn. Not with this one."

"What do you mean?"

"I'm not looking for trouble, but this one's trouble." His words, so matter of fact, only confused her.

"How do you know that?"

"In prison, the P.O. factor is big talk. In fact it's the one thing we're constantly talking about when we're told we're going on parole." He sounded weary, and cynicism etched his words again. He went on, wanting her to understand, "We know, for instance, that there's two hundred and twenty-five P.O.'s in this city, and we know *all* of them by name. We know who we're going to have if we live in lower Manhattan, who it's to be in Queens or Bedford-Stuyvesant in Brooklyn, what each and every P.O.'s reputation and attitude is to ex-cons, who's fair and who's foul. Well, Robyn girl, I've drawn a bastard!"

"Oh, God. don't go in there thinking that!"

He shrugged. "Fact. Green Haven and the other

prisons are full of repeaters—men and women who've been broken by P.O.'s like this one and sent back for 'violations.' So, that's life."

"It could be different from what you expect."

"We'll see."

"It's *got* to be!"

A uniformed officer, sitting at a small desk inside the entrance, told both Robyn and her father to sign their names in the daily register; also date and time of "Admission," and their business in the building. Robyn saw the carefully groomed black officer look her father over, staring at his brand-new shoes longest, before accepting his transfer papers. Then her father painstakingly wrote down:

"March 20, 6:35 p.m.—Robert Adam, reporting from Green Haven Prison to parole officer."

Robyn signed below, as "visitor, accompanying father." The officer then ushered them inside a rail to the small public section near some desks with black-lettered signs taped on them: "ARRIVAL OFFICER." Several men and women, none in uniform, worked at the desks from large manila folders, now and then calling someone over from the public section. On the brown wooden benches, Robyn and her father sat waiting with other ex-convicts and their relatives.

Except for the occasional ringing of a telephone, or an Arrival Officer's calling a name out, a dead silence pervaded the room, and Robyn felt that she knew the smell of fear. Her father sat up straight and rigid, as though in school, or, she thought sadly, still in some prison cell. She sought desperately to make him relax.

"The plants are pretty, aren't they? Those jonquils . . . they're the color of my new sweater that Mom . . ."

He cut her off abruptly. "Yeah, I grew them inside. Gardening was one of my jobs."

Was he only tense, or was it the mention of Mom? She sat beside him now as silent as he. His name was called, and she watched him stand up uncertainly, then go to a desk. His Arrival Officer was a woman, chunky and grey-haired, quite motherly, Robyn thought. After checking through a folder and asking him something, the woman telephoned someone. Robert Adam sat straight and waiting, listening to the woman, staring ahead of him after she hung up. Minutes later, a large, muscular, shirtsleeved man, bald-headed and deeply tanned, stepped briskly off the elevator and went to her desk. She saw her father stand up then, saw the woman introduce the two, heard the man say in a cool, authoritative way, "Come along then, Adam."

Robyn got to her feet. She crossed swiftly to where the man was leading her father to the elevator. Her eyes were on the parole officer as, instinctively, she caught her father's arm. She drew him aside, and kissed him as the officer watched.

"I'll wait here, Daddy."

"That's my girl."

"It's wonderful that you're back," she said loudly.

"I'll be down soon, dear."

"Okay, Adam," the man said tolerantly.

He was with the parole officer for nearly an hour. Robyn left the bench only once, to buy herself a Coke from the coin machine. When he returned, he looked pinched and withdrawn. Without a word, he motioned to Robyn, and they signed themselves out and left the building.

They walked in silence for blocks, and now he seemed oblivious of the street life and traffic. She burned with curiosity about his encounter with the P.O. but accommodated herself to his mood. He would talk when he was ready, and she tried not to feel confused.

Just before they got to the Holy Apostles Center near Twenty-eighth Street, where he was to stay temporarily, he finally let it burst out in accents of agonized disgust: "It was like I told you!"

"What did he do?" she stammered.

"It was worse!"

"Tell me!"

"Why? What good will it do?"

"Tell me! I'm not a child!"

"Oh, baby, not a child?"

"I have to know what we're up against!"

"*We?*"

"That's right. *We!*"

"A rotten deal, baby, that's what! This P.O. said . . . listen to this . . . he said, 'I don't give a damn what you think about me. This is what *I* think about *you!* I think you're an asshole because you became a problem to your family and to society and to yourself, and *to that girl downstairs!* So don't think you're going to be a problem to me because I'm going to throw your ass right back in prison!' That was what he used for openers, baby!"

His voice had dropped to a self-pitying whimper, but the words stung. "I didn't say anything, Robyn, I swear. I just sat there, taking it all, worrying, but that seemed to provoke him worse than anything because I wasn't reacting. So he kept at me: 'Look, this is your first day out! And if you don't want to go back in, this is what you'd better do. Get a job! Don't get involved in any crimes! Stay away from any bad influences! Don't take a drink! Don't hang around with any other parolees! Don't hang around any dame who's boozing or on drugs!' He was badgering me, and I knew it, and I was trying to stay loose, but I thought I'd better say something so he'd cool it. So I said, very quietly, 'What are you talking about, man? I just got out today. That's my daughter downstairs, who's helping me to find a decent place to live and a decent job. You know from my folder that I've *got* a job lined up.' But he just went on—trying to scare me. 'I know your kind,' he said. 'You're up to no good! I know your *thoughts!* It's just a matter of time till I see your ass back in the county jail and then prison. You know, you did *kill* someone!'"

At the sound of the dread word, Robyn felt an old sickness pinch the pit of her stomach. But she kept silent, letting him pour it out: "Honest, I tried to stay loose but

I could feel I was getting angry, and I didn't want to raise my voice—that could be a violation—so I held in my anger and I said, very controlled, 'Look, man, you're a stranger to me! I never met you before in my life. Why are you going at me this way?' Know what he said, Robyn? 'You don't have to know me,' he said. *'I'm in control of your life now, man!'* After that, all I remember saying—I don't know how many times—was 'I don't want to do anything that would put me back in prison.' Robyn, do you understand what I was doing? I was . . . I was *groveling* before him!"

They were at the Center.

Robyn felt drained from the day's ordeal, and unequal to the strange and terrifying new experiences. But she held back her emotions as she told him, in a tone that sought to counter her father's self-contempt and bitterness, "So he gave you a hard time. He's just one person. There's plenty of people, maybe here at the Center, maybe on the job, who are not negative. You'll see."

"I have you, Robyn girl."

"You'll have other people, too, who care."

"Wanta bet?" She caught the self-pitying note again in his voice. Again the despair, the cynicism, as he said, "People are afraid of ex-cons."

"Maybe."

"Why aren't you?"

"What?" His abrupt question startled her, really shook her, and she answered him, trying to make a joke of it, "Should I be?"

"No, dear, of course not. I mean, not of me." He kissed her cheek sadly then. And for a fleeting moment, she was remembering the handsome hero-father of her early childhood; full of laughter and stories, he was "a lovely man," people said warmly. She had adored him; but what did that "lovely man" have to do with this haunted, fearful, broken ex-con beside her now?

"Does your mother know where you are?" he asked suddenly.

"Mom?"

"And her husband . . . and the rest?"

"No."

"Are you going to tell them?"

"If they ask me."

"I'm being a burden to you, Robyn. I don't want to be a burden to you."

She let her dammed-up confusion and tears come out then.

"For God's sake," she cried, "you're my father!"

2.

On Ninth Avenue the gracious, rambling old church with its well-trimmed front lawn was an anachronism in that dreary area of the city—like a serene, green-treed oasis. Its Center, a halfway house for men making the transition from prison to the outside world. was a few steps down in the church basement. The door was unlocked, another warming touch. The quarters inside were inviting: a games area against brick walls, painted sky-blue; beyond, several couches, club chairs, and a small library of paperback books near a television console; beyond that, some offices.

At a green-baize pool table, a couple of men looked up as Robyn and her father entered, smiled at them. and went on with their game. Father and daughter walked to the office area, where a huge, beefy black man with snapping eyes and a short, bristly beard welcomed them in booming tones.

"Hi. Robyn . . . this your father?" He shook hands with them. "I'm Johnny! Well. man, how does it feel to be out? How was the trip down?"

"It was okay."

"Good. Anything special you want. right now?"

Robyn saw her father's eyes widen in surprise.

"Want? Well, now that you ask . . . yeah. I think I want to go and stand by the river. Just look at it again."

Johnny roared with laughter. He understood.

"And so you can. But stick around a bit first—I have to start this weekly meeting. Nothing formal; just my way of letting the guys ventilate their feelings—and tell them

13

mine. Give you some idea. Meantime, take a look at that Notice on the wall."

He moved off to get the men together, and Robyn and her father read the Notice, printed large, and straight to the point:

> This Center is not too proud to admit that there are situations that we are not able to handle. This is a residential program for a maximum of *twelve weeks,* for men released from prison on parole—and who want to remain outside!
>
> We see ourselves as a decompression chamber, bringing an opportunity for a new life outside prison. This program was started by a parolee from Dannemora prison, and among staff there are other parolees. They know it's a tough scene to leave prison with just 40 bucks, no job, no guidance, no decent place to shack up. We provide this initial help so a man can get himself together.
>
> There's really no catch if residents behave responsibly. But if a parolee thinks the Center would be a good place to lay up for a month or so while he looks for some gig to get into—
>
> *HE IS CORDIALLY INVITED NOT TO APPLY!*

"How did you hear about this place, Robyn?"

"Accidentally—that day when I visited you at the prison, from a woman visiting her husband. Johnny helped me to draft your parole plan. And he wrote the prison that the Center guaranteed to take you in here initially."

"So that parole officer—I've forgotten his name already ...no, Mortimer Locke ... *knew* you'd arranged this?"

"It's in your parole plan, in your file with him."

"But he said, don't hang around parolees. That's what he laid on me, remember?" His voice was coldly furious.

"But he knows he can't go by the book if you come into a Center like this one," she protested. "Everyone's a parolee here."

"The bastard!" he spit out. "He could 'violate' me already!"

"He can't! I'm sure he can't! Even Johnny is a parolee, and he heads all the counselors here! The P.O.'s must know that."

"You think so?"

"Of course! Ask Johnny!"

The angry flush, reddening his face and ears in his turmoil, began to subside. He turned with Robyn to listen to Johnny, who was opening the meeting. Some twenty men, ranging widely in age from early twenties to late fifties, stood against the pool table or sat near the silenced television. The men aired their complaints and hopes, and Johnny listened and nodded and took notes. Someone complained that the showers weren't working in the upstairs dormitory. Another said he was out of pocket money, provided by the Center, to look for jobs, because his first job guarantee had "flopped." The big man questioned him about the efforts he was making, took notes, gave him some words of cheer. Another man said his time was almost up at the Center, but now he needed help on housing: his job at the car wash had folded; he had nowhere else to live. Johnny took more notes.

Others began to speak up—they were running into similar problems with jobs and housing. One man's family had moved from New York and he wanted Johnny to help him find his wife and children.

And one young man, listening to the others for a long time, spoke up with a groan, "Listen, man, I've got no job, nowhere else to go, and I'm tired, man. I want to go back to jail!"

Now Johnny, who'd been letting the ex-convicts—burglars, thieves, policy-runners, muggers—run on about their problems, threw down his notes, and began to roar at them in language no one could mistake:

"Don't tell me 'I'm tired'! You wanta go back to jail, go back to those mountains! *GO*! No one's stopping you! But just remember, there's no one in this room done more time than I have! I've done seventeen years myself! I've robbed, stolen, pimped. I used to know one thing only—how to pop guns and how to bullshit! But I will not bullshit you in any way! I'm a *square* today! I work till midnight here every day of the week! My ex-wife is into me for five thousand dollars alimony, but I'm not about to do time to get it to her. Don't you tell me, 'I'm tired'! You wanta go back to jail—man, you can go! But that's a sucker move! *OKAY, MEETING'S OVER!*"

The big fellow mopped his brow and looked around, glaring at his audience. There was an immense silence in the room, but one or two grinned up at him sheepishly. Robyn, pale and nervously excited by Johnny's speech, sensed that the men hadn't resented it, since it came from one of their own, a peer. She stole a look at her father, and he seemed tormented. Johnny crossed to them, and reacted to her father's appearance.

"Look, Robert, you've had a rough day. Seen your P.O. of course?" Wry smile from Robert. "Yeah, well, we know his sort, but just hang in and stay strong. Now, here's a set of keys to let yourself in and out of the Center. You can take your bag upstairs to the dorm. We'll talk in the morning."

"Johnny, I want to thank you . . ."

"I understand, man. Don't forget. I'm here because someone gave me a break a long time ago. Your old firm's promised to take you back, right?"

"I guess so. I'm not entirely sure."

"So tomorrow, we'll see if they keep their word."

Johnny shook hands with them again, his hearty manner veiling whatever worries he had about the job.

"The man's incredible," her father muttered, looking at Johnny's receding figure with awe.

"One of those people I meant . . . who cares," she said quietly.

He changed the subject. "Robyn girl, aren't you expected at home?"

"I'll be all right. Let's have that coffee . . . talk . . ."

"No, no, listen to me. I appreciate everything you've done, but, you know, I meant what I said to Johnny. I really would like to go and stand by the river. Alone. You do understand?"

"Yes. Yes, I think so."

"We'll have a long talk, very soon."

"Like tomorrow."

"Tomorrow? Can you come?"

"Of course! I'll want to know about the job. And I have to go over to the apartment, and let you know when you can move in."

He held his daughter to him then for a long moment.

When she left, she realized that he hadn't asked her any details about her mother.

3.

It was quite dark, past nine thirty, when the bus delivered Robyn to her neighborhood. West Eightieth Street, where she lived on the sixth floor of a high-rise apartment house, was already eerily deserted. People weren't venturing out much after dark on the side streets, because of the rise in street crime.

In the spacious, old-fashioned apartment, with its high ceilings, the bay window festooned with plants, the imitation marble fireplace with brass andirons, the shelves of knickknacks, the upright piano in splendid isolation within an archway, Robyn let the protective skein of familiar surroundings draw her in. The stark contrast of it all with the scene she had just left down on Ninth Avenue was overwhelming. She was also aware that she was very hungry.

She saw her parents, watching television in the dimly lit living room; the table lamp, outlining her mother's pretty, youthful face and well-groomed blond hair, made her seem curiously neon-tinted. A night baseball game was on, and she sat immobilized in the big old club chair, sewing something while her husband watched the game. Looking so deceptively small and vulnerable, Robyn thought with a pang. Her mother put the sewing down and got up at Robyn's entrance, but George Grenshaw barely sent the girl a look before turning back to the game.

Ethel Grenshaw, with set jaw, marched toward Robyn who was making for the dining room-kitchen area. Joyce was doing her homework on the fragile, Queen Anne desk as usual. Ethel deplored such use of the lovely piece which could barely support a plant, but she never ordered Joyce away from it; the desk had belonged to Joyce's late mother, and been in her family for ages as had the piano, the Dresden pieces, and the heavy, mahogany furniture which filled the living room.

"Hi, Joyce," said Robyn.

"Hi," said Joyce, who was a year younger. She didn't look up as she went on, with disdain, "Watch out for Ethel."

Robyn saw her mother wince at the tone.

"Please don't talk that way, Joyce," said Ethel.

"What way?"

"You know what way."

Joyce looked up then, staring coolly at mother and daughter. She adjusted her dark-tinted, aviator glasses on her puckish, upturned nose, enjoying the advantage of staring openly at people who couldn't see her eyes; then she jerked her shoulder and turned back to her work.

"Robyn, where've you been till this hour?"

"I meant to phone you, Mom. But there was no chance. I'm sorry."

"I asked where you've been."

"I had to keep an appointment, in town."

"With whom?"

"Well, not with Victor," Robyn said, stalling.

"We know that. Victor has been here, looking for you. He said there was an editorial meeting . . ."

"Oh, wow . . . I forgot!"

"You forgot something so important?"

"It happens, Mom, it happens!"

"So . . . where were you?"

"Mom, I'm hungry. I'll tell you, later."

She nodded warningly in the direction of Joyce.

"Not later," said Ethel. "Now."

"No."

"Not with Joyce here," Joyce piped up. Ethel ignored the interruption.

"And I said *now*!"

Her mother's voice had been rising, something that seemed to astonish Ethel as much as the girls. Ethel liked to say she despised loud, angry voices which meant a lack of self-control and breeding, and her voice was generally as smooth as her hair and nails. But now she was failing her own gospel.

Robyn shook her head miserably. She was confused by the events of this day, wanting to share them with her mother, but fearing reprisals or, at the least, misunderstandings; she was certain her mother would want privacy for this talk. The common tragedy they both shared had long schooled Robyn in ways of holding back; so she simply stiffened now under her mother's angry probing. Her head began to throb worse than before, and she wondered if that was what people felt before they collapsed from hunger—or guilt.

"Mom, I absolutely have to eat something."

"Supper's finished."

"I don't want much."

"You're not going to tell me?"

"It's just that I'm so hungry . . . got this headache."

"Okay, then, let me tell you, Robyn."

"Tell me? What?"

Joyce spun around now to watch mother and daughter in earnest.

"I wouldn't want you to lie to me."

"I wasn't about to!"

"I know that you've been with . . . with your father."

Her mother's voice was shrill, menacing.

"Oh? How'd you know that?" Robyn stammered.

"She's been in your room." Joyce put in calmly. "She read some letter and showed it to Dad."

"What? You didn't!"

"After Victor came, and you weren't home, I was worried, so I went to your room. I'm not ashamed!"

"I can't believe it!"

"Not only I! *We* were worried, both of us. We like to know where our girls are!"

"Well, bully for you!" Robyn said, coldly. "And have

you done this before, Mom? Have you read my mail before?"

"No." But Ethel Grenshaw's voice was uncertain.

"I'm seventeen! I have a private life. A very private life of my own! Anyway, I was going to tell you."

"But away from Joyce," the girl said, insolently.

Robyn stared at her stepsister. Suddenly, like some tortured reaction to the day's confused events, she grabbed off the other's oversized glasses, wanting, she felt, to smack Joyce's face; instead she found herself looking into eyes filled with instant fear, and she hated her impulse. She threw the glasses down on Joyce's homework, and said grimly, "Why don't you fuck off!"

"Robyn, how dare you use such language?" Ethel shrilled.

"You're shouting, Mother."

"Don't you criticize me!"

Robyn gave a short, bitter laugh. "What made you do such a sneaky thing? Read my letters from Daddy."

"Your daddy's dead! He is to me! He should be to you!"

"So you always said."

"But he *is*!"

"Now you listen to me," Robyn said, struggling to remain calm. "My father, Robert Adam, came out of prison today. He told me that, at the prison gate, they handed him forty dollars and a paper to give his parole officer. He is now on parole, after being shut away for six years. You listening, Joyce! Taking it all in?" she added, deadly calm, not caring now who heard it. Including George.

"You mean, *Robert's been dead* for six years!"

"Not to me, Mom!"

George Grenshaw had been standing at the entrance for several moments. A shaggy man of medium height, with short, curly black hair streaked with grey, his usually humorous black eyes now drawn with pain, he viewed the commotion with distaste.

He was production manager in a noisy midtown firm, a business-opportunity publishing house, and he looked for-

ward to coming home to a quiet, stable apartment, which
it usually was. He liked nothing better than TV of an evening, watching his favorite spectator sport, with a pipe
and a beer, and he had no patience with scenes. They
tended. he said, to put him off his appetite and sleep, and
that, he joked, could give him a nasty split personality.
Now he stared unhappily at the scene between mother
and daughter.

He certainly hadn't bargained for this when he had remarried three years ago, after the lingering illness and
death of his wife, Joyce's mother. Ethel, a secretary at the
time in the firm where he worked, whom he married pri-
marily (he told himself) to provide some stability for his
young daughter, had, in fact, proved to be a grateful and
devoted homemaker, while continuing with her office
work. He shared his gratitude for that openly with both
Ethel and Robyn, and knew that he had Robyn's respect:
he had told the girl, early on, that he knew about Robert
Adam and the divorce; he said earnestly that they—the
four of them—were leaving their respective tragedies behind them and starting a brand-new life together, as a
family.

But Joyce, whom he loved the most. had been far from
accepting. He often wondered. he told Ethel, if Joyce
could do something about her appearance—the youngster
was overweight and seemed, even to his loving eyes, careless and dumpy by comparison with Robyn's graceful
good looks.

Whatever the reason for the present commotion, one
thing stood out most for George Grenshaw. His evening
was ruined. He hesitated. though.

He rarely came between mother and daughter; indeed,
there rarely was any reason to, for usually they were ex-
ceptionally compatible. But from the harsh exchange he'd
now heard. he didn't want the "ghost" of one Robert
Adam in his house either.

Wasn't Ethel quite right? She had divorced her first
husband while he was in prison; since he was a felon. that
made him "civilly dead" to the family, under the law; and

they could begin a new life for themselves as though he were really dead, which Ethel had done (and very bravely, too, thought George). Just the same, there had been times when he'd speculated whether they might be confronted one day by this high-spirited girl who had adored her father. (Didn't children, even those given away for adoption, often go looking for their real parents after they grew up?)

Something in the human psyche . . . some overpowering curiosity about them . . . the need to find one's roots—to know?

Now he tried to remain detached.

"Robyn, you're upsetting your mother." he said. "Why don't you go to your room. We'll talk this out later, all of us."

"That's fine with me. I'll just make a sandwich, okay?"

"It's *not* okay," said Ethel, but her voice had dropped with George's intervention. "We have to know what you're planning. Where you're going to be tomorrow, for instance."

"Now, Ethel, she'll tell us . . ."

"We have to know, George. I won't risk . . ."

"But, Mom. you can't forbid me to see him. That's what you're getting ready to do, aren't you?"

"Yes!"

"Well, don't!"

"Robyn," said Ethel, on the verge of tears, "why are you *doing* this to us?"

Robyn gave a start. The whole. strange day, with its potpourri of fearsome characters and nostalgia and elusive motives and doubts suddenly fell into place with her mother's words . . . the self-same words, she was now remembering, she had asked herself in the long-ago past: Why is he *doing* this to me? Have I done something bad? Why are you going away? Why are you *doing* this to us? She was only eleven at the time . . . the years had blurred his image but not her own words of accusation.

Remembering now, she said softly,. "You should understand, Mom, he never asked for my help. I offered it."

"But why? Why involve us?" This very quietly from George. The girl saw that her stepfather's hands, hanging stiffly at his side, were clenching and unclenching, and she sensed his frustration and worry. "Ethel is right, you know. We don't want the whole family drawn into *his* situation." And he added carefully, not wanting to hurt anyone, "The man is nothing to us, Robyn."

She stiffened. "The *man?*"

"Now don't go dramatizing things," Ethel cried. "You're always dramatizing everything! So he was your father."

"*Is.*"

"Well, well," George said dryly, "I thought I tried to be."

"Oh, George!" Robyn crossed to him then, and kissed his cheek. "You're so good, and you're the kindest man I know. Won't you try to understand?"

Joyce was watching them with a mixture of surprise and disdain, and in the moment, George seemed to relent. But Ethel intervened angrily, "Understand what? I know you even went to see him in prison, without telling us."

"How *could* I tell you, Mom?"

"And now this!" Ethel rushed on. "*And* wherever else you've been today with him. I suppose you think you're being idealistic or something!"

"It was . . . something I had to do," she stammered.

Ethel kept on, in her fear and unhappiness: "Had to do? Rubbish! I suppose you feel heroic or something, fishing in those old, stinking waters again! I won't have you bringing that *stink* in this house!"

"Mom . . . stop."

"And . . . and there's Joyce as well as you to think about."

Ethel was deliberately touching a raw nerve in George with that one; but the younger girl only sent her father an enigmatic look. Robyn caught the look. She could guess at some of the real fears which were influencing them: the old newspaper stories; the social disgrace; the revulsion of friends; the rejection by neighbors following the scandal.

Now, her head throbbing with confusion, but angry, too, with the way her mother was impugning her motives, she suddenly wanted to be done with them all for a while. The day's events had been trauma enough.

"Do me a favor, Mom," she said roughly, and she saw her mother grow rigid, ready to strike back again. "Just be quiet!"

Then she brushed past Ethel and George and ran to her room.

She lit the small lamp on her desk, and looked around the room, trying to visualize her mother's incursions here, feeling somehow dirtied. Her portable typewriter, her cassettes, her leather ring binder with notes about the coming term paper were on the desk, undisturbed. The lowest drawer, however, was shut tight in a way she never bothered to leave it. She swallowed hard: the drawer contained her most private and personal mail.

For a while she stood just inside the door, staring around, seeing anew the dark purple wall behind her bed, hung with Chagall and Picasso prints, and Victor's sketch of their beautiful holiday in Provincetown. The wall, contrasting with the rest of the white-painted room, had been a sudden idea as a backdrop for the prints; Joyce had approved of it for her own odd reason: "Very sexy color, that," she'd said quite civilly. The walls of her own room remained a faded pink, and bare except for a large, framed photograph of her mother.

Robyn undressed, and brushed her hair, hoping that the strokes would ease the throbbing. She got into bed, and tried to focus on Victor, to shut out her mixed feelings of grief and guilt, but it didn't work. She kept coming back to the old, accusing words: Why is he *doing* this to us? So, who was right in this family drama? Herself? Her mother, who implied that her motives were less than pure? Both? Whose values were to prevail? She closed her eyes, aware that her empty stomach was not a good psychological adviser.

Then she remembered the gift box, still untouched in her tote bag on the bureau. She got out of bed and car-

ried the box back to bed with her. She took off the birthday wrappings and sampled a Sulta Nut Meat. It was
sweet comfort, and she took another.

She leaned back on her pillow, and felt her bitterness
begin to decline. She no longer struggled against the day
and her thoughts—would Victor characterize her adven-
ture as only an ego trip? Well, had it been?

She let old memories flood her mind, and felt she was
watching the pieces of her life pivot and collide, as though
staring into a slowly turning kaleidoscope. The pieces
took one shape, then another, shifting . . . changing . . .

4.

Easily, her happiest memory was a time of the long ago when Robert Adam had packed her and Ethel into his company's station wagon and driven them down the East Coast for holidays in the Florida Keys—the chain of tiny islands between the Atlantic and the Gulf of Mexico. She was nearly eight.

That summer her father had returned from Vietnam, decorated, he said wryly, with a Purple Heart and a shell fragment in his left shoulder, "buried in me forever."

The real estate firm where he had worked since college days had contributed its own reward: a month's paid vacation. And since he planned to spend it in Florida, his boss broadly hinted that he should look over some properties there of interest to the firm. A Vietnam hero was no mean property himself, the firm's president had written smoothly, urging Robert to wear his uniform and medal until his formal Army discharge. Robert ignored the cue. He'd been an unwilling recruit in a war which he'd despised, he told his wife and daughter, and he not only doffed his uniform but also gave the medal to the person who had made such a to-do about it: his mother.

Robyn remembered it had taken a whole week just to drive from their Greenwich Village apartment down to Florida. Ethel was navigator, and her road map was gaily red-circled with places of interest. Except for visiting her parents in Denver, she'd seldom been out of New York State; and now she wanted to see "everything."

They began with Independence Hall in Philadelphia, where the Declaration of Independence had been signed in 1776, and the Liberty Bell which had rung out that news on July 4. After that gusty experience, she had navigated them through Washington and the White House; led them to the top of the great, marble obelisk of the Washington Monument; and, of course, to the halls of Congress. They left the car to go bicycling along the Potomac River, Robyn riding in tandem with her father.

Robert had his way completely in the Blue Ridge Mountains, though; they spent two restful days in an isolated lodge, read stories, took long walks, and closed out the world. Driving down the coast into the Deep South, they had loved their first glimpses of the palms, the exotic, showy hibiscus, and the tropical gardens growing with lush extravagance. With Robyn sitting between them, Ethel and Robert kept the radio going with songs and weather reports; and, laughing with happy intimacy, they deliberately switched off all the news. They were in a world of their own.

In Key West, her father rented a bungalow not far from historic Martello Towers, the old fort from pirate days which dominated the seaport. And life for them on the sun-drenched naval base was informal and lazy. She learned that the colorful town was a favorite of artists and writers: Ernest Hemingway and Tennessee Williams had homes there, and former President Truman had owned his "Little White House," set behind the great palms.

Now, while her mother indulged her historical interests, exploring the town and its architecture, Robert took her on quiet drives in the Keys, or for picnics on the beach, or among the gnarled fishermen for some offshore fishing. Street vendors would pass with their cries and whistles— *"Mani, mani, tostado!* Toasted peanuts, five- and ten-cent bags!"—and local and Cuban boys hawked jelly pies. Robert would toss them coins, or buy something. Other times, the three of them would go up the stone staircase of a little café, high above the town, and have cool drinks and food on the balcony while gazing at the Atlantic Ocean.

The picturesque town and the people were ambrosial to

them, at first. But there were times when Robert fell silent, like a conch withdrawing into its shell. (Ethel would tell her later that it had to do with his war experiences.) Then her father would stay out late at night, drinking rum or beers in the oak-beamed tavern which was a favorite of strange characters from the mainland and Cuba. He would stagger back to the bungalow, sometimes frightening her as he bumped noisily into things, and sleep it off next day.

She remembered Ethel remonstrating at last, "Keep this up if you want to ruin our vacation!"

"You're too serious!" he would reply, rumpling her mother's hair, and laughing infectiously. "Life's too short to take seriously!" He told her not to worry, it wouldn't happen again. But it always did.

Before they left Key West, he remembered to examine the waterfront properties for his firm, which was to please his boss and lead to some very profitable sales later.

Those were the good memories, green and fresh.

Back in New York and at work again, Robert was different. He seemed restless, melancholy; and he drifted back in earnest to the drinking habit he had acquired in the Army. It began to affect his work and their home life. Ethel and Robert quarreled nearly all the time now it seemed; and Robyn would cower in her bed, hearing the abrasive exchanges. In the equally dreaded silence that followed, she would wonder in terror: What's he doing to my mother?

Sometimes after a quarrel, he would come into the bedroom, look down at her in his melancholy way and say, "Sorry, baby," or "It's all my fault. Don't be frightened." Then he'd disappear for the evening, saying he was going to his mother's house; or he'd go to his "Club"—the Village Bar and Grill—in search of the euphoria he seemed to crave.

The quarrels took on a new dimension after her grandmother, Robert's mother, remarried.

Robyn loved her Grandma, who always had some surprise waiting in a hidden place for her to find. A Dublin-born, plump little woman with snapping, bright blue eyes and frizzy red hair, she had an amazing zest for life and people. She had migrated alone to America, was widowed soon after Robert was born in New York, and worked in various shops on Long Island, to "stay clear of Welfare." A very proud and independent woman, she was able to send her son to college on her savings and scholarship aid.

Robert doted on her. He liked to boast to Robyn that Grandma was really "la grande dame of Dublin," while Grandma, of course, relished telling everyone, with a dash of Irish wit, that she'd "climbed up from the mucky slums of Dublin-town to the mucky slums of Elmhurst, Long Island!"

But she kept her apartment as neat as a pin, with an open door to her friends, and an open mind about her mixed Irish and American ways. She always had a "hearty man's meal" for Robert when he came, like corned beef and cabbage (though she said she hated the smell of cabbage), boiled potatoes and leeks, fresh-baked soda bread, and her wonderful deep-dish apple pie. For Robyn there were puddings smothered in whipped cream.

Grandma's house was always alive, it seemed to the child, with love and music, with Grandma singing away as she put the finishing touches to this or that dish. Sometimes Robyn asked why she didn't have a husband, like Ethel; and Grandma would flush and murmur something then, but Robert would swing his mother around, give her a big kiss, and shout boisterously, "What for, when she's got me?"

So he was understandably shocked—"disgusted" was his word for it—when Grandma suddenly remarried, and announced the event to them. Her new husband was a construction worker, toughly handsome, with coarse, pocked features and a tattooed chest, and he was several years younger than Grandma. During her parents' talks about this startling event, it was hard to tell what Robert hated most: her marrying a much younger person, or the man himself.

As a result, their visits to Grandma's became fewer. But the times that they did go, Robyn remembered only that the man had a mop of black hair, laughing eyes, and very strong arms that tossed her up to her delight; and that Grandma, watching the horseplay with affection and bursting with energy herself, always served him first at table.

As she grew, Robyn shrank more and more from the arguments between her parents following the visits:

"What do you mean, married beneath her!" said Ethel, with a touch of maliice. Her own parents, retired school-teachers, lived in a fashionable garden complex in Denver.

"So she has."

"Don't be stupid. She works, and he works."

"It's disgusting! Don't you see?"

"What?"

"She just needed someone to love after I got married. She was lonely. He took advantage of her loneliness."

"Oh, come on, Robert, for heaven's sake . . . !"

"Sure, it's true."

"You can't be serious! She loves the man."

"That what you call it?"

"He's her choice, that's all I know."

"Don't you want to know what's going on there?"

"Going on?"

"He *hits* her!"

"I don't believe it!"

"Believe it."

"Did your mother tell you that?"

"I've got eyes in my head."

"But did she say that, Robert?"

"I tell you, she doesn't have to!"

"How do you know then . . . ?"

"Christ, it's not something you talk about!"

"But she'd have said something!"

"Not my mother! She's too proud!"

"You mustn't interfere!"

"Don't tell *me* what to do!"

"But, Robert, she loves him!"

"He's just a cruel bastard!"

"Maybe he is. Maybe he's doing what you think. But with some women . . . anyway he's what *she* wants! Can't you get that through your head?"

Her father's eyes would cloud over, and the irises grow dark with some inner anguish. He'd look away from Ethel, and send Robyn a funny, twisted smile before charging out of the apartment after such an argument. She and her mother knew where he would go: to the "Club."

During that time, Robyn grew to fear the tension between his disappearances and returns. He would come home very late, stumbling yet full of energy, talking loudly, his hands trembling, trying to control them, making weak jokes: "I'm a free human being, you're a free human being." Or "Never met a woman I didn't like, Ethel." And cracking flippantly from the Bible, which seemed to irk her mother the most: "It's a time to love . . . time to hate/A time of war . . . a time of peace!"

Sometimes, he would vomit, then seem to fall asleep, then shudder and vomit again. He could be whimsical. Once he stole a bunch of chrysanthemums from a garden near Sheridan Square, and when he presented them with a deep bow to Ethel, she said tartly, "Hot mums, is it now? Better hide them from the cops." He thought that very funny, and roared with laughter.

In stony silence, her mother would get him undressed and into bed. She slept with Robyn those nights.

His work suffered as his drinking problems grew.

He complained about his shoulder wound, as if the pain were responsible for his slacking off and the drinking; but the wound to his pride seemed to be far deeper, and he was like a boat stuck on a sandbar. He was acting as though life had mistreated him: he said he'd killed and seen his buddies killed in the war, and seen thatch-roofed villages razed, and farmers turned into homeless refugees, and he couldn't forget that—or the fact that he'd returned to a job which was meaningless to him. He said he felt

"cheated by life." That was the way he went on in his sober moments, his self-pity masquerading as philosophy.

Quite often now there would be the smell of alcohol on
his breath at breakfast, which made Robyn wince as he
bent down to kiss her good-bye; affecting not to notice
that she'd pulled away, he'd crack, "Have a good day,
baby; your daddy can lick anyone on the block!"

"Big deal," her mother would respond grimly.

Ethel feared his going to work that way. She'd heard
from his secretary—"I hope you won't mind, Mrs. Adam,
I'm embarrassed to have to inform you . . ."—that they
were concerned about his drinking, and unless he did
something about the matter . . .

Ethel told him straight.

"You know what it is—I hate the job. Should have
gone on to law studies after I came out of the service."

"So go to law school nights. Other veterans do!"

"Too tired nights," he replied lamely.

"Too drunk you mean."

"You don't understand."

She hurled at him, "Why are you *doing* this to us?"

"Doing what?"

"Do I have to spell it out, in front of the child?"

She would cry. Robyn would run to her, feeling sick
with anger because her mother was crying and hurt;
feeling, too, a nameless agony over her father's frustra-
tions. Her fears were growing, and once she burst out at
him, "I hate you!"

"Don't ever say that, darling," he had responded, with
a melancholy smile.

Afterwards, there was always a sort of truce, a strange
modicum of peace during which her parents stopped talking to each other altogether. In this time, he turned more
and more to Robyn. When he could, he took her to Central Park, bought her binoculars so she could be "a real
pro" like the other bird-watchers; he helped with her
homework; read her poetry and stories, and had her read
to him. He taught her to play chess (always managing to

let her win); and he took her to Broadway plays and musicals, the way, he said, he used to take his mother.

He rarely went to his mother's house now.

At ten, Robyn was intensely curious about all the places and people and music and poetry that he was opening up to her. They usually went alone on their trips, Ethel saying she preferred to sit home and watch television. And Robyn, feeling very grown up, loved those special times with her father.

One evening, she slipped over to the "Club" to be where Robert stood drinking at the crowded bar with a group of men and women. At first, he was pleasantly surprised, and began to introduce her as "My girl . . ." but then his mood changed, and he swiftly paid up and took Robyn outside.

"Never do that, baby," he chided.

"Why? You go there!"

"It's a den of thieves," he began to joke. "No, not that," he added hurriedly, "but it's not for children, you understand? Especially with homework waiting!" And he hugged her and smacked her bottom playfully. "Don't tell your mother you came! She'd be very angry. Okay?"

They kept it secret.

But there was no secret about the deterioration of Robert Adam at work.

Then when she was nearly eleven, he disappeared from home for several days. He'd never done that before.

Ethel telephoned his office. A secretary told her, with some sadness, that she had thought Ethel knew that her husband "had been let go." Her mother frantically telephoned around—no, he hadn't been back to the "Club." His mother hadn't seen him, and "is anything wrong?" Ethel replied, "Probably not. Keep in touch."

Tight-lipped, holding in her emotions, she began mechanically to clean the whole apartment as though getting ready for some festive occasion.

"What's happened to Daddy?"

"I don't know."

"Isn't he coming home?"

"I don't know."

"Mom?"

"Yes, Robyn."

"Shouldn't we phone the police?"

"No, no, no police! Just go to school . . . keep your mind on your work, like I'm trying to do here. We'll hear soon enough."

They did. But not from the police.

Grandma telephoned, her composure gone, weeping hysterically, imploring Ethel to "please come . . . I don't want to be alone!" Robert had been there, yes . . . there had been a terrible accident. No, she didn't know where Robert was now, but "I'm so desperate. My husband . . . he's dead!"

Ethel left Robyn with a neighbor, and went to be with her mother-in-law that night.

The story made all the papers next day.

A classmate brought the morning *News* to school, and, nudged on by others, he dropped it on Robyn's desk. With shock and fascination, she looked down at a dramatic picture of Grandma which showed her kneeling beside "her dead husband . . . killed by her son." She heard nervous titters behind her, as she began to read the story: Following a brawl, the son, Robert Adam, "in his drunken rage," had hit the other so hard that the man's head had struck the iron radiator, and the man had died instantly. Now the son, a war veteran, had disappeared, apparently unaware of the consequences of his blow; he was being sought by the police, and was asked to give himself up.

The story was clearly the sensation of the class. Of the whole neighborhood.

She came home white-faced and crying, and her mother held her tight when she said no one wanted to play with her. Her mother took her out of school that week.

She telephoned her parents in Denver about the "social disgrace," asking if she and Robyn could stay with them a while. They replied no, absolutely not, they certainly wouldn't want to ge involved in a murder case, there would have to be a trial, they were respectable, decent people, and didn't she realize . . . ? Her father, a fundamentalist who taught Bible studies, was still rattling on as Ethel quietly hung up.

"What are we going to do, Mom?"

"Move. Go to another neighborhood. Another school. Start fresh, Robyn," Ethel muttered, trembling and desperate.

"What about Daddy?"

"What about him?"

"How will he find us if we move?"

But her mother only shook her head in a bewildered way, and kept saying, again and again, "How could he *do* this to us?" All her efforts from that moment, it seemed, focused on trying to spare Robyn and herself from being stigmatized.

They moved from the Village to the upper West Side. Ethel had Robyn transferred to a new school, and registered her under Ethel's maiden name of Milford.

"Robyn, forget the 'Adam'—you're now Robyn *Milford*. Say it, darling. Get used to saying it! We have to break with the past. We have to make new friends!"

"But what about Betsy? She's my best friend."

"What about her?"

"I have to see her. I miss her."

"Did she want to see you, play with you?"

"No."

"Did she say why?"

"She said her mother didn't want her to."

Ethel held her close. "It's all right to tell Betsy where we're going to live if you like."

But though Robyn slipped a note with her new address under Betsy's door, Betsy never came.

5.

After Robert gave himself up, Robyn remembered, her mother seemed to be dressed in black all the time. She had to attend his trial in the Criminal Courts Building in Manhattan, but she kept all the details of that terrible period to herself. She never took Robyn to the court-house; she told the girl that the judge and the attorneys, both prosecuting and defense, urged her "to shield the child; there's no need for her to be here." When once or twice, in her intense curiosity about what was happening to her father, the child tried to ask questions, Ethel reject-ed them, saying abruptly, "Forget it!"

Grandma went to testify at the trial; then she went out of all their lives, completely. She packed up, closed her apartment, and returned to her native Ireland.

Ethel never brought a newspaper into the house now; and she forbade Robyn to read the papers. No one knew her background at the school, Ethel said, adding, "We have to make up our minds to forget the old life, Robyn. I'm putting it all behind me, once the trial is over; and you must!"

But Robyn couldn't forget. She was confused.

"How's Daddy going to find us at our new address?" she cried.

"He's never going to find us, Robyn. Stop asking!" Ethel answered sharply, as if to shake sense into her.

"But will I never see him again?"

"He's going away, very far away."

"Never coming back, Mom?"

Ethel said, her voice quiet but trembling with anguish

for both of them, "*Never*. Not to me, not to us. To me, it's as if he really died after he left Grandma's house that night. He's not the same person he used to be. So I feel he's dead, Robyn. And you have to accept that, too."

"How can I, Mom? *Why*?"

"Because he is never coming back, Robyn. That's the same as dead!"

And that was the way Robyn had to accept things, especially after Ethel divorced Robert Adam while he was in prison. She had taken a job—as Ethel Milford—with a Manhattan publishing firm, and told Robyn that one day she hoped to return to college and earn her teacher's certificate.

After she married George, they went to live in the Grenshaws' gracious apartment. Robert Adam, his heinous crime and the social disgrace had, until a year ago, become a fading memory. The father she had adored had simply gone out of their lives, leaving no trace. Or so it seemed.

Part of her mind was relieved that her mother had worked out their new life so successfully; but the other part, especially as she grew into her teens, secretly craved to see and touch Robert Adam, to find out what had really happened. Still, it remained buried in her subconscious until that day, a year ago, when her stepsister, Joyce, had viciously raked over the old ashes.

The younger girl had practically thrown a tantrum when Robyn told her that she and Victor Burnside and a bunch of juniors were going for a holiday weekend to the Burnsides' summer home in Provincetown. Joyce was furious at being left out.

"Wants to be a doctor, like his father, doesn't he?"

"I think so " said Robyn.

Joyce said, needling her, "No skeletons in his closet—yet."

"What does that mean?"

"Nothing."

"Victor's no skeleton. He's merely beautiful," Robyn said dreamily.

And the other had cut in spitefully, "Well, see how love and murder will out!"

Robyn had gone pale, and started toward the other, but the younger girl had backed off, muttering, "We're studying Congreve. He said that, not me."

"And now you're saying it. Why?"

"You *know* why."

Robyn said evenly, "Okay, so I know. How much do you know?"

"About what?"

"My father. What else?"

"I know he's a . . . a criminal!"

"And how'd you know that?"

"From kids who knew you in your old neighborhood. Ethel always told me he was dead!"

"He is, to *her*. Anyway, this doesn't concern you."

"Oh, no?"

She knew that Joyce wouldn't let the matter drop. But the hateful episode was not without merit, she told herself: It had forced into the open. for her to face at last, the questions which had lain dormant for so long—too long: Where was he? What had he really done? What was happening to him now? Was he alive or dead?

In some powerful way, her mind at least was reaching for him again. for the father she had once adored . . .

She confided in no one. But after they returned from Provincetown, she went to the Criminal Courts Building in downtown Manhattan, where she remembered he'd had his trial. In the information office of that tall, concrete-and-steel "Court of Record," a clerk took notes as she described her errand: to locate her father, Robert Adam, who now was aged thirty-eight, who had stood trial in this courthouse back around her eleventh birthday.

The clerk was a white-haired. sedate. and patient black man, who tactfully kept his head down while she described her father's crime from the old newspaper story. He told her to have something in the coffee shop downstairs, while he got the information for her from some old records.

After she returned, he was able to tell her that Robert had been given a ten-to-fifteen year sentence on a reduced manslaughter charge (instead of the more serious Murder-1), because the killing "had not been premeditated, or with use of deadly weapon." That he was in Green Haven State Prison in upstate New York. And that to get permission to visit him, she must write to the Commissioner of Correctional Services, in the State Office Building in Albany, New York.

He wrote the address down as he advised her of procedures, adding with a smile of encouragement, "Albany always gives permission to the immediate relatives. He'll sure be glad to see you, miss."

As she thanked the clerk, the most overwhelming feeling she had was that of guilt—guilt that, with her innate, consuming curiosity, she had not long since sought out the truth for herself!

She wrote to Albany for the permission. And she wrote to her father, holding back her deepest emotions:

Dear Daddy,

> *I hope this finds you well. I've only just learned where to write to you, and soon, I hope, to visit you. I shouldn't have waited so long, but I'll save the explanations until we meet. I'm sixteen now, but in some ways, I guess I'm still the "little girl" who took a present to the Queen.*

> *With love,*
> *Robyn*

She gave her school and homeroom as her return address. He wrote back, on blue-lined, copybook paper, that the best present he could have in his whole life was her letter and her promised visit. And she had gone by bus upstate on a Saturday soon after, to visit him alone, in secret.

She had rationalized that seeing her father was a private matter; but in her heart, she knew she didn't want to face the censure of her mother and the Grenshaws, and, quite possibly, that of Victor Burnside. Not just then.

The memories, old and new, were getting mixed up in the kaleidoscope. The colors were at an ebb, and the serrated pieces, shifting and changing more and more, seemed to move into shadow. At last, Robyn slept.

6.

She had awakened after a restless few hours of sleep, with the same headache she had taken with her to bed. She squinted at herself in the bureau mirror, and her reflection only added to her woe.

"Ouch! Do I know you?" she asked it dolefully. "You look like your unmade bed, Robyn Adam!"

In a sort of pact with herself, after she had visited her father in prison, she had privately been trying out her real name; she hadn't used it publicly since she was eleven.

The emotions of the previous day began to rekindle in her, and she stayed longer in her shower than usual. But it didn't help. She couldn't put down the sure knowledge that she was in for another bizarre day. What was the anodyne for it? She felt confused as she dressed.

The apartment she had found for her father was obviously not suitable—too close to home for Ethel and the Grenshaws, and perhaps Robert himself. An alternate must be found; she'd have to do something immediate about that; maybe she'd have to lie to her father about the reasons for that changeabout . . .

Mechanically, she began to brush her hair, the rhythmic ritual of long, hard strokes. She tried to turn her thoughts to the school play and her lines for it—she had a major role in Arthur Miller's drama *The Crucible,* the historical play about the strange and shameful witchcraft fever which seized the Puritans of Salem Village, Massachusetts, in the 1690's.

She was cast as Abigail Williams—Abby—ringleader of the young girls who gathered in the woods to listen to an Indian slave tell them wonderful, forbidden stories of magic and witchcraft. Then, fearing terrible punishment in the village for their actions, the girls began to accuse many innocent elders of practicing witchcraft on the children. Their lies led to the elders' hangings on Gallows Hill outside the town of Salem.

In that strange epidemic, the youthful accusers, led by Abby, eventually managed to fill all the prisons of Salem, Boston, and Cambridge with their victims. The fever lasted for sixteen months; then as suddenly as the hoax had begun, the fever was over, and the executions ended, with one jury praying for forgiveness for its mortal error.

In Miller's notes, which Robyn had studied with interest, the playwright wrote that such a witch hunt—in modern terms, the persecution of one's political opponents—can happen in any age where there is repression of human rights. People had to rise above individual villainy, he wrote.

The role of Abby was a tremendous challenge. Robyn had wanted to make that Puritan girl's vindictiveness very compelling. But now, as she brushed away rhythmically, she felt morose and unequal to such a role: Abby was just "too heavy a burden" in her life; she didn't like her lines; she was in her own crucible, wasn't she?

She would have to write about it that way to her drama coach, asking for a less demanding part. Yet she was loath to disappoint the coach who had such confidence in her acting, and who also said that Robyn "had the voice."

"You know, some girls have the sort of voice that people want to run from," she had said. "Yours has what I call 'staying power.'"

This morning, trying to lean on her coach's belief in her staying power, Robyn placed her largest book on top of her head, pulled in her stomach and rump tightly, and marched up and down her room, rehearsing, however, not Abby's lines but the things she planned to say to the landlord.

She fervently hoped that the man would stay long

enough to accept her explanation about the apartment, and be persuaded to release her from that obligation.

She wore the yellow outfit which Ethel had bought for her birthday, wanting to look her feminine best. She had a real-life part to act with the landlord, she told herself; and then there was Victor, waiting in the wings.

She had to face, at last, just how much she would—could—tell Victor. They had been going together in this last year of high school, and were college bound; recently she had begun to wear his school ring. What was *he* going to make of all this?

Would he shun her, despise her? Would *she* be a victim of guilt by association? She started to visualize what life would be like without Victor . . . without her girl friends and the drama coach . . . remembering how she had once lost her best friend, Betsy.

"Just cool it!" she told herself out loud. "Mom's right—you're always dramatizing everything!"

Ethel and George had already gone to work when Robyn went for breakfast. Joyce sat at the kitchen table, shoving moodily at her cold cereal and skim milk (she was on a well-publicized, high-protein diet this month, to shed a few pounds again) and Robyn tried to ignore her as she warmed up the coffee.

"Ethel gave me a message for you," said Joyce.

"Yes?"

"She said, 'Tell her definitely to be home after school unless she has a rehearsal.' "

Robyn nodded.

"You going to be?"

"I don't know."

Joyce eyed the other through her aviator glasses. Flat-chested, chunky, her corn-colored hair hanging to her shoulders like candy floss, she seemed to be deliberately exaggerating her bad points with her oversized glasses and sloppy clothes. Yet the dark-tinted glasses, which nearly filled her face, hid her best feature: her large eyes, which were wide-spaced and of an incredible bright blue, luminous and intelligent under thickly fringed eyelashes. They stared thoughtfully at Robyn through the frightening glasses.

"About last night, Robyn."

"Well?"

"You know . . . about Ethel . . . your letters . . . ?"

Robyn waited, drinking her coffee.

"I wanted to say I'm sorry."

"For what?"

"Just sorry, Robyn."

"Forget it. It's my problem."

"I only wanted . . ."

"And I said forget it!"

"It's just that . . . I couldn't sleep," the other blurted out. "and, well, I don't know why, but sometimes I can be such a stupid bitch!"

And before the astonished Robyn could react, Joyce ran from the room. She left for school, banging the door after her.

Robyn looked at the unfinished cereal. She slowly finished her coffee, and decided that some good had come out of last night's mess after all: Joyce had never seemed so human to her before.

She would have to hurry.

She thought sadly: And there's no way I can avoid another scene with Ethel, maybe George, too. She had to see her father later, hear about his first day at work, tell him about the apartment. The promise to him, she felt, had priority. Which meant coming home late, and another—what was her coach's word for a mess on stage?—farrago. The word always got a laugh from the cast. There was no laugh in this real-life episode.

She went looking for the landlord.

The apartment, on which she'd placed a fifty-dollar deposit from her savings account, was near her high school, close to home. Only last week she had fantasized that she and Robert would have an easy "bachelor pad" to take care of, easy, too, for her to reach. The events of the previous night had washed out that prospect; now she must get her father and herself released from any financial responsibility for it; and his P.O. would have to be told.

*   *   *

The landlord lived in the converted brownstone, and he met Robyn on the stoop. He was a big man, Falstaffian and bearded, with a roll of fat bulging over his loosely belted trousers. He carried a clipboard on which he made notes, as though each controversial word meant a threat. He looked at Robyn's pretty figure, and seemed at first as ingratiating as when she had given him the deposit. She began to explain.

But he said promptly, "Can't make any refunds!" After all, he went on, couldn't he have rented the place ten times over during the past week, when he'd held the apartment for her? He scribbled something on the clipboard, said he'd now have to put back the "For Rent" sign. He figured (figuring on the clipboard) he'd already lost money on this deal. What was wrong with the apartment, anyway?

Robyn tried desperately again.

"It's just that my father . . ."

His manner changed, his voice becoming strident as he hugged the clipboard to his hefty bosom and surveyed her.

"I'm being very liberal, girlie, letting you off your agreement. And how do I know he's your father, eh? I mean, you're under age. You got a mother, girlie?"

Robyn fell back, a sickness beginning to pinch her stomach. Her head throbbed. The man said, leeringly, "Could be he's someone on parole? We get some of those. Cops wouldn't like you mixed up with that, know what I mean?"

"We didn't have a contract," she stammered.

"You give me a deposit. That's a contract in any language. A non-returnable deposit, girlie."

People on the other stoops were listening to the exchange, and the man's loud, accusing tone. The color drained from Robyn's face.

"I'll need the deposit for another place. Please!"

"Listen, you wanta change your mind, okay, but no refund! Get it?"

"But my father needs an apartment in another area!"

"Tell your father to come see me!"

"No! You don't understand."

Confused and frightened by his attitude, she backed off and bumped into a garbage can. The lid clattered to the ground, and one or two little kids tittered, but the adults on the stoops and passing by gazed stonily at her. She held her books tight, and walked away.

Let him pick up the old lid himself!

Dirty-minded old man!

Stupid people, staring, making her feel guilty about something!

"Can't win 'em all," someone called after her.

She didn't look back. This was her neighborhood, but she felt alienated, suddenly back in her old neighborhood and the remembered hostility. She kept her head high as she walked away, imagining that she was walking offstage, but not to any applause.

She felt very sick about losing her deposit.

It was unreasonable, perhaps, but she felt robbed.

7.

"Hey, you look very nice, I mean, dangerous in that outfit. Who're you trying to charm anyway, Robyn?" Victor began with a short laugh.

"Charm? You. Who else?"

"What for? I'm all yours!"

She grinned with relief. She'd gone and dramatized things again. Victor was just his relaxed, bantering self.

"My idea of saying I'm sorry . . . about yesterday."

"That's okay. But *you* called the meeting, you know."

"How did it go?"

"Well, it didn't. You're the one they really depend on for ideas, sparking their young minds." They laughed. "When you didn't show,"—he blinked once or twice through his heavy, horn-rimmed glasses—"I adjourned the meeting to this afternoon. You might say I panicked!"

"You panic . . . never!"

"Well, so I goofed off."

He was still smiling, but silent now, marking time as he remained in his chair, his long legs draped over one arm of it, waiting for the girl to explain.

They were alone in the large, spacious office, which was partitioned into cubicles, provided to editors of the various school publications. Bulletin boards adorned each cubicle, with glossy pictures of student staffs, rehearsal shots, page proofs of the coming Yearbook, and a host of large-lettered, pointed legends:

"Life is a jest, and all things show it,
I thought so once, but now I know it."—John Gay

"The optimist sees the doughnut,
The pessimist, the hole."—McL. Wilson

"We . . . would rather die on our feet, than live on our
knees."—President Roosevelt, address, 1941

"Do unto the other feller the way he'd like to do unto you
an' do it fust!"—E. N. Westcott in *David Harum*

Victor and Robyn co-edited *The Beacon*, the monthly
literary magazine, with Robyn more the manuscript editor,
selecting the stories and poetry, and Victor the supervisor
of art and business matters. A sudden slump in submis-
sions from students had led to yesterday's emergency
meeting with staff.

In the late afternoon, the place would be a hive of ac-
tivity in all the cubicles, but at the moment, they had it to
themselves. Robyn hesitated before Victor's quizzical
smile, wondering if his present mood fitted her own, and
her escapade. A darkly handsome fellow, with short, jet-
black hair, and probing, lively brown eyes under heavy
brows, Victor Burnside was probably the most admired
senior in school: clever at everything, in sports as well as
class, ambitious but self-disciplined, planning a medical
career like his father's. Mostly he was famous for his
"cool timing," which Robyn found rather awesome: in
class discussions, he liked always to time his own contribution after all the other comments were in, clearly enjoying the impact his ideas made. Not all his classmates
shared Robyn's feeling about that attribute, some scorning
it as "a sharp device to get attention," or "just a snob
thing." But there was never any doubt that they waited
for Victor's "turn," and it was usually worth waiting for.
Sometimes shattering, Robyn thought.

She grew tense now under his well-known silence. He
saw her tension, which puzzled him. So he undraped himself, and came around the desk and held her in a warm
embrace.

"What's the matter, Robyn?"

He kissed her gently on the mouth. Then he pushed her away gently, asking, "So what's your problem, kiddo?"

She stared at him a moment. Then she said in a small, determined voice, "My father came out of prison yesterday. That's why I couldn't be at the meeting."

"Your father *what*?"

"Came out of prison. My real father, Robert Adam."

"'*Adam*'?"

"That's my family name . . . I'm Robyn Adam. I was named after him." She heard herself enunciating each syllable carefully, letting them drop like pebbles against her brain.

"You're telling me that your father . . . a guy called *Adam* . . . has been in prison?"

"For the past six years. Since I was eleven."

"I see," he said quietly.

"I don't think you do. But, anyway, I had to go to the bus terminal to meet him. He came out on parole."

"I see."

"For God's sake, Victor, stop saying that! How can you . . . till I tell you about it?"

"Well, why haven't you up to now?"

"I don't know."

"What, er, had your father done?"

"Well, I'm not exactly . . . I think he may have killed someone."

"Good God!"

"I've been told he was very drunk at the time. Didn't know what he'd done even."

"Who was killed?"

"His stepfather."

The silence in the room became oppressive. Victor tugged unconsciously at his glasses and shook his head in a puzzled way. Suddenly, Robyn was aware that his voice, still cool, had hardened.

"Well, I seem to remember you said your father was dead."

"I'm sorry. I used to have to say that."

"Why?"

"I was told to. My mother . . . we were afraid."

"You could have told *me* the truth."

"Maybe I should have."

"Maybe?"

"It's not something you want to talk about."

"Want to talk about it now?"

"Yes. Please!"

He nodded. "Okay."

"Could you get some coffee, Victor?"

"Sure. Back in a moment."

At the door he paused. "Should we call off the meeting this afternoon?"

"No, don't do that. But I won't be able to stay very long."

He stood pondering that, turning her reaction over in his mind, then he shrugged and went for the coffee.

She gazed after him, wondering where to begin, how he was going to take it. He was the one, above all others, she felt she could turn to; she could talk freely now; she certainly had his love and trust. He would understand why she had to act privately during the past year. He would understand and support her . . . surely, he must, she told herself fervently. I need someone to share this with at last. Someone with ideas, to help me . . .

"It all really started for me again just a year ago," she began after Victor returned with containers of black coffee. "I think I kept pushing into the back of my mind the fact that my father wasn't really dead. I always had a burning curiosity about what happened long ago . . . but, you know, he hurt my mother so much that I think there were times when I was little when I *wished* he was dead! Then my stepsister, Joyce Grenshaw, you know her . . ."

The other nodded silently, sipping his coffee.

". . . she hinted that she didn't believe my mother, who always said Robert was dead. She'd heard he was in prison . . . for murder." She stared at the boy miserably. "I had to do something about it then . . . find out things for myself, Victor, now that I'm grown up."

He held his silence, but Robyn was used to that, and she hurried on, all the drama of seeing her father now flooding her mind. "He was in Green Haven Prison in up-state New York, they call it maximum security; and no one had ever visited him there."

The boy looked at her with steady, troubled eyes, and she trembled as she drank deeply from the container.

"Why did you pry open that old can of worms, Ro-byn?" he said. "Your mother did make a new life for her-self, and for you . . . didn't she? A better life?"

Robyn was startled at the sharpness in his voice.

"It must be instinct, makes you do certain things," she replied. "Anyway, I wrote him, and he wrote back that he wanted so much to see me. He wrote he could never for-get me."

"So you went to the prison?"

"Just once. After that visit, he wrote he didn't want me to come again. Said he worried about its effect on me, be-cause I told him about that."

"What effect?"

"It was the *Wall*!"

"The wall?"

"It was awful! This immense, thirty-six-foot, towering wall, surrounding that whole concrete cage . . ."

"Prison, Robyn, prison " the boy interrupted coolly.

She stared at him, her eyes glittering, seeing the wall again . . .

"Cage to me," she said deliberately. "The wall at Green Haven has concrete watchtowers and guntowers on top, at spaces all around the roof. You can see the uni-formed guards moving inside the watchtowers, with rifles pointing in all directions, and looking through binoculars. It's all so medieval, Victor, and right in the middle of the most lovely countryside. Hard to imagine unless you've been there! Because before you get to it, everywhere is serene.

"The bus takes you through villages and green hills. There's lots of streams and sheep and cows in the valleys, and white horse-fences, and very old trees which come right down to the highway. It's like a storybook picture, the setting! Then, when you're completely unprepared, there's this crazy, concrete wall, rising up and cutting across the whole horizon. Like a great, grey wave . . ."

"We have to put prisons somewhere," Victor put in, very crisp and cool. She bit her lip.

"The bus takes you right up to the wall, and the entrance. Some convicts were putting in plants along a walk, and they didn't look up when you got out. Like they were afraid, or embarrassed, or something."

"Don't dramatize," he said.

"Now you sound like my mother!" she retorted. But he sent her a faint smile, and she continued, "I shouldn't have told Daddy how I felt about it, especially the wall. He didn't know about the keepers roaming it with their guns so openly."

"Go on. What happened inside?"

"Even the visitors are made to feel like prisoners! It's strange but true. You go through this big iron gate, then a metal detector, and everything is clanging behind you as gates open and shut. Your handbag's examined, your lipstick taken apart, the date is stamped on the back of your hand . . ."

She indicated the upper part of her left hand.

". . . so they can recheck that when you leave the place. The guards take down the name and number of the person you're visiting; check how many visits the prisoner has already had. Everywhere you feel the suspicion, as if the visitors aren't human! I don't care," she flared up, catching Victor's quizzical look again, "that's the way I felt! Everything is gates and guns and keys and . . . and contempt!

"Then you go through another iron gate to what's called the Visiting Room. In fact it's about the size of our gym. There's a horseshoe-type table that fills the big room. After a bit, inmates come in and they go inside the horseshoe; visitors are on the outside. Guards here and there, watching everyone. It's terribly crowded, no privacy. Everyone is speaking at the same time, so you kind of cup your hands close together, like this, and lean across the table, and try to speak into each other's mouth."

"Gruesome," said Victor in a tight voice.

"Remember, I was seeing Daddy for the first time since I was little. Oh, God, Victor, if you knew how I had loved him . . ." Her hand went to her mouth, but she was quite steady when she spoke again.

"It was so strange. At first, we just sat and held hands across that table. Everyone was chattering or shouting around us to make himself heard. We just sat and looked at each other. Then he said, like he'd been thinking about it for a long time, a rhyme which he knew I'd remember . . . about a little girl who'd been to visit the Queen. It's just an old nursery rhyme, but it worked, and we laughed then and started to talk at the same time. He looked so different, very thin and pale, but when he laughed that old laugh, I knew my Daddy! After that, it was so fantastic, Victor, to be able to touch, to realize that he wasn't dead. He wasn't! In fact he was being recommended for parole."

"You shouldn't have made that trip alone, Robyn." The boy's dry comment cut across her memories, like some neutral editorial comment on a student essay. The brittle tone shook her, and she drew back.

"It was something I knew I had to do! That's all. He told me he was counting the weeks and days when he could come out. Said he'd written to hundreds of firms, like other parole candidates, names they got out of the telephone directory; because they need what they call an assurance of work and a place to live, before the Parole Board grants parole. And no one had answered him. Can you imagine?"

Victor remained silent, and she could only wonder about that as she hurried on, wanting him to imagine and understand. "He asked me to find some halfway house in New York which could intervene for him, perhaps with his old firm. He said, above all, would I keep writing to him, now that we'd found each other again?"

"Did you tell him about me?" asked Victor.

"No."

"Why not?"

She stiffened at his tone, and said, "I didn't want to involve you, I suppose."

"But I am involved! Aren't you my girl?" His voice was light, bantering again. Still she felt a stab of uneasiness. "Don't be so damn protective," he said.

"It's just, I can't help feeling he only has me."

"There you go again, Robyn, dramatizing!" the boy said testily. "Don't forget, he did kill."

She drew in her breath sharply. "*And* he's paid for that. Hasn't he? He'll have to go on paying for it for years, that's what parole is . . ."

"He may even be dangerous now."

"What's that intended to mean?"

"Just this: I suppose it was all right for you to see your father in prison, but you don't owe him a thing."

"I owe him . . ."

"What?"

"Some understanding . . . help. He seems so . . . afraid."

"Of what?"

"So many things."

"He should be. Could deter him from ever doing . . ."

He caught her look and stopped his rough tone in time. But he was confused, and the exchange had left both of them drained.

Robyn had hoped that the frankness between them would bring them closer than ever; not only because of their common interests, but also their shared belief in "being involved with humanity." Now, though she had involved him, she felt curiously alone: in fact, she seemed to see a wall like that of Green Haven rising up between them, separating them.

She wanted desperately to put the feeling down.

"Now it's out in the open, well, this is just between us, isn't it?"

"Of course," he said abruptly. "Stay after the meeting. Let's talk some more about it."

She said, "I can't. I have to see my father. It's his first day at work, and I must help him find an apartment."

"Want me to come with you?" No longer abstract, the boy sounded sincere, eager to help.

"Thanks, Victor, but not yet."

"Why?"

"I don't think he's ready for too many new faces. But I'll tell him . . ."

Victor's face went very pale and set. He stuck his hornrims on top of his head and studied her.

"Don't be angry!"

"Angry? Who, me? What a funny girl you are!" he said, trying to joke. "Where are your vibes, Robyn? Can't you see what a great frame of mind I'm in?"

She gave a nervous laugh. She stuck his glasses back on his nose, and kissed the tip of his nose.

"You're beautiful, Victor Burnside," she said.

"So what else is new," he cracked back.

But he picked up his books, and left the room without another word.

And later that day, at the editorial meeting of *The Beacon,* when Robyn made an excuse for leaving early, she saw Victor's head go down as he busied himself with papers. She could only guess at his feelings.

"See you tomorrow, Victor?" she asked.

"Sure," he replied, without looking up.

8.

Robyn noticed the difference in her father at once. In contrast to the edgy person of yesterday, Robert was remarkably relaxed, his face animated as he hugged her.

"What a grand day I've had, Robyn!"

He took her to the office where Johnny, the black director, hailed them, and tactfully left them alone there.

"Everything's going to be fine! I got the job!"

"That's fantastic!"

"Not my old job, you understand, but in the same place."

"What does it matter!"

"Right! And my boss said not to worry—he'll be the only one at the office who'll know I'm on parole."

"So he kept his promise."

"He did, he did! Robyn, you know when you come out of that damn cage, *survival* is the game. You can't win without a job. He kept his promise!"

"Fantastic!"

"So you keep saying," Robert laughed, and in the moment the laughter reached his faded eyes. "Can't do it alone. You helped. Johnny helped. That's what did it! So many guys who earn parole, plead and badger and pray that someone on the outside will at least *promise* a job. The promise alone works to get them released. Then they're paroled and the promise turns out empty."

Robyn shivered. "No one to help them."

"People are afraid of ex-cons and parolees. They've been burned too many times; the country's not too concerned with the released con." He banged his fist into the other palm. "Me, I got lucky. Bless you." His voice was husky. "I'll earn a hundred dollars a week, it's about a quarter of what I used to make; but at least it gets me going again. Robyn, my boss actually created this job for me, he said."

"What do you do on it?"

He hesitated, and the smile became strained. "Well, it's menial—clerical work, sorting the mail, some filing, locking the place up after hours, things like that. Not exactly, uh, creative, is it?"

"So what? Did he promise . . . ?"

"My old brokerage job? No chance." He went on quietly, "You have to be bonded and licensed for those jobs, and parolees are all on a so-called disability list. Meaning ex-cons are barred from a lot of skilled and professional jobs."

"I don't understand."

"Well, those of us who once worked for banks or real estate firms, or even drove a taxi or tended a liquor bar—all the categories, Robyn, which require a State license—are usually barred from them under that 'disability code.' Because the jobs involve trust and money, and contact with the public."

"But that's so unfair," she cried, "when you're trying to rehabilitate yourselves!"

"Maybe. But it's the law." He shrugged. "If you get a certificate of good conduct through your Parole Officer, or when you come off parole finally, you can try to qualify for licensing and other civil rights. Trouble is, that can take years."

"How many years, Daddy?"

The smile had vanished. "The rest of my sentence probably . . . nine years."

He went on, "I guess that's why Johnny got so uptight at the meeting last night. That old disability code seems to program ex-cons for failure right from the start. The men get frustrated, especially if they don't have work, and get into trouble again with the cops. I've seen them—repeaters—coming back again and again to Green Haven."

"But not you!"

"Of course not, love," he said. "I need to move out of this Center, though, and get on my own feet again. Tell me about the apartment, Robyn."

She stammered, "I'm so sorry, Daddy, but it's not ours, after all. Anyway, you wouldn't have liked that one."

He waited for her to go on, as though quite used to bad news, expecting it now.

"It was dreary, and the street was very scruffy."

He took a deep breath. "What you're really telling me is that the place was too close to Ethel, okay?"

It was the first time he'd mentioned her by name, and his cynicism made her mother another presence in the room, watchful and hostile. "Did you catch it from them last night?"

"It was nothing," she said evasively. "I just couldn't take the apartment. That landlord was a goon!"

"But what am I to do?" He sounded faraway and suddenly fearful. "My P.O. knows we had some apartment waiting. He said he was coming to look it over, part of regulation number something-or-other."

"Tell him the place wasn't satisfactory, and we're looking. You can stay here for some weeks, you know . . ."

"The less I have to tell him, the better, Robyn." The fear tightened his face again.

"Daddy, he'll understand!"

"He'll think we *lied*."

Robyn stared worriedly at her father.

His shifting moods were alarming, and she realized how little she really knew about this gaunt, fearful stranger, separated not only by years but by dreadful experiences. She wished that Johnny hadn't left them alone—he was better able to cope with such moods and problems. Maybe the director would know about living quarters close to the Center. On the other hand, would her father resent that sort of advice as an intrusion? He had said pointedly that he wanted, more than anything, a private life of his own.

She said gently, "Come on, let's eat something."

She took his arm, and they walked the few blocks to Frank's Coffee House, which catered to the Center's residents. There were few people on the street at the dinner hour, and his gaze now moved in awe over the ivied gardens that fronted some majestic old brownstones; in fact, they discovered a brass plaque at the corner, stipulating this as "a landmark street of historic interest."

He paused to look back at the well-tended houses which, like the church, resembled an oasis in the otherwise seamy neighborhood. "It's hard to believe that there are lovely places like this, right in the heart of the city," he said. "I'd almost forgotten."

In the small, crowded coffee shop, they chose a booth just inside the door, and Robyn shook off an eerie feeling that the nearness to the street had some psychological significance for her father. Johnny was eating at the counter, and after a moment's hesitation, her father signaled to Johnny to come and join them. As the big man did so, Robyn was aware that a skinny, pallid little man, gnome-like, with staring eyes and tufts of hair showing on his chest through his open shirt, followed behind Johnny, and he slid into the booth's fourth seat.

Johnny said with a short laugh, "Meet Olaf the Stick."

"Hello, Johnny," Olaf the Stick said, in a voice that whimpered.

"Just know, my friends," said Johnny, "wherever you find Johnny, the Stick can't be far behind. That is, when he's not back in jail. Right, Stick?"

"Go, Johnny, go!" the Stick said eagerly.

"Got a job now, haven't you?" The Stick nodded. "Like a tag along until you're busted again?"

"Not gonna get busted again, Johnny. Not if you help me. Just don't send me back to Bayview, is all I ask, Johnny! Who's the broad?"

"Don't call her that!" Robert burst out, angrily.

"Oh, it's all right, Daddy," Robyn said. She was secretly excited by the strange human assortment in the coffee shop. Johnny put in calmly, "Stick, this is Robert, who's living at the Center for a while, and his daughter

Robyn, who's visiting us. Now stop the smart-assing, and say hello nicely to the lady, Stick."

Johnny's earthy reaction to Stick brought Robert down an octave or two, which was clearly Johnny's intention. The Stick said fervently, "I'm sorry, we don't often see such beautiful dames—oh, Lord, Johnny!—ladies where I come from!"

"No, really, it's all right," Robyn protested, with a schoolgirl giggle, wringing a faint smile from her father.

Johnny said, "Everything okay today, Robert?"

"Couldn't be better, for a start."

"Good. Then we're on the right track with you."

"Thanks to Johnny, right?" the Stick said in his whimpering voice. "I'll just bet Johnny did it! Always remember, stay close to Johnny if you know what's good for you. Know how old I am? Take a guess, go on . . . fifty, fifty-five? I'm *thirty*! I been busted so many times, I'm already sick of life. But Johnny here, he always picks me up again! But Johnny, just don't let them pack me into Bayview again!" he pleaded.

The waitress came for their orders, and Johnny concentrated on his burger as Robyn and her father asked for the same with French fries. Johnny remained quiet, an oblique encouragement to the Stick, whose compulsive verbal flood seemed a form of therapy: "I'm bitter, I don't mind saying I'm bitter, Johnny. About my last arrest, I mean. It was for a two-dollar bag of horse, which I didn't even have on me. The cops planted the sale, Johnny, I swear it. They're always watching me, I've been busted so many times. You know they've got to fill this quota of arrests, so I'm a sure snatch with my record, Johnny.

"Only this time, they sent me to Bayview when I came out of prison, supposed to be a halfway house, but it's a chamber of horrors, no better than another prison! Like you come from work, and they make you get back into prison-issue clothes inside. There's bars on the windows like prison, and paper plates to eat off and no forks, and no *trust*! Trust, Johnny . . . that's one thing you never get in there!

"So listen, I've packed my shower clogs and shaving cream and toothpaste and toothbrush and towel, that's all I've got to my name, and it's with me, and I'm taking myself out of there to the Center. And oh, God, Johnny, if you boot me out of there . . . ! Listen, man, I'm desperate, don't send me back to Bayview! You've got to help me again, man! Please help me, Johnny!"

They were listening to the Stick, watching him, in tense fascination. Robert sat rigidly through the assault on their feelings, hardly breathing, as though sharing the Stick's desperation, but warding it off.

Johnny said, "Eat up, Stick. You're not going back to Bayview."

"Oh, man, you won't regret it, Johnny! Oh, man, I'm never gonna get busted again!"

"Eat up, Stick," Johnny said wearily.

"I don't know why Johnny let him go on and on," Robert said irritably as he took her to the Eighth Avenue bus. "I don't want you listening to all that garbage."

"I've heard it before."

"You have?" he asked, surprised.

"I mean, there are even kids at school who've been busted."

"Well, you're not to mix with that lot, hear!" Then he collected himself, blurting out in a self-mocking way, "My God, look who's ordering you around!"

"Oh, come on, Daddy."

"Well, who am I, trying to manage you?"

"It's okay."

"I took it too personally, didn't I?"

"I like you to be concerned."

"Boy, what a grand girl I've got!" And his smile shone again, radiant and pervasive, touching her deeply. The moment seemed right to tell him about Victor.

"I've a friend, he's very special, Daddy, wants to meet you."

"Special you say?" The smile wavered, and she saw him stiffen as though expecting a blow. She hurried on.

"He's really . . . you'll like him. His name's Victor, in my graduating class, and we've been going together all year."

"He knows about me?"

"I told him just this week."

"Why did you have to do that, Robyn? Why spread it around?"

The whimpering tone, that she'd also heard in Stick's monologue, was back in his question, like an accusation. It confused her. "But Victor had to know, Daddy. We're going together, we share things, we . . . love each other." He fell silent.

He was still pondering that as they got to the bus stop. "It's okay, you did right," he said at last. His mood had shifted again, and he seemed under control. "Bring him around to Frank's if you like, Saturday evening; we can have coffee and . . . get to know each other."

"Great, Daddy."

They talked then about her work at school, her part in the play, the new search for an apartment. And suddenly Robert said he'd decided to try to locate near the Center . . . be quite near Johnny, "until I'm really on my feet again."

So the Stick's monologue had penetrated his consciousness more than she'd realized, thought Robyn. There was a lot to be said for some "garbage."

It was late again when Robyn arrived home, and she was dreading another confrontation. In fact, Ethel and George weren't there. Joyce announced from the TV corner, in a tone distinctly offhand, "Ethel's furious with you, and Dad took her to the movies."

"Is he very angry, too?"

"Would that bother you?" The cynicism was back in Joyce's attitude.

"Since you ask . . . yes, it would."

Robyn stared, frowning and troubled, at the back of the other's head. She found herself wishing passionately that her stepsister was someone she could share some things with. For a moment, that morning, Joyce had seemed different—almost human, she had thought, when she made that crusty crack about herself. But here she was again, as withdrawn and distant as ever. Turning up the TV more loudly, deliberately.

To wall me out.

Making me feel like an outcast.

The way I felt earlier, with Victor, so walled out from him.

And from Mom.

Oh, stop dramatizing that damn wall!

Victor's on your side—didn't he say he was involved?

And George *would* be, if he were let alone.

As for Joyce acting so superior . . . there was another side to her; she'd seen it.

Anyway, she told herself with an unexpected bitterness that surprised her, "She's got something to feel superior about, hasn't she? *Her* father's not an ex-con."

9.

She had cut her early morning class for the two previous days, and Miss Carnovsky motioned Robyn to come to her desk. She had entered with the others amid the usual, noisy excitement of students coming together again with bits and pieces of their own private lives; and she realized that with her new world gone topsy-turvy, she hadn't thought through her explanations for her absences. The teacher eyed her searchingly before asking, "Will you stay after class, please? I want a word with you about the term paper, and also the school play."

"I'm so sorry, Miss Carnovsky," Robyn began.

"Later, Robyn," the teacher said, adding dryly, "but I am glad you're gracing the class with your presence today," a smile softening her irony.

One thing about Carnovsky: when she put you down, she did it with that smile. If there was one person in school with whom Robyn felt complete rapport, it was with this English and dramatic arts teacher. She was so comfortable to be with: a tiny, youthful woman, with saucer-round, intensely grey eyes and fluffy grey hair, dynamic-appearing in her well-cut slacks suits, but very feminine, too, with her long, silk scarfs making splashes of color on her shirtwaists, or used in lieu of a ruler to make a point.

Carnovsky had a mysterious background. Some said she was a descendant of a Russian princely family, the Rostoffs; others, that she had worked with American intelligence against the Nazis during World War II. Victor told Robyn that he heard she came from a Polish musical family, had managed to escape from a German concentration camp, and was brought to England and to America by a relief committee after the war. Carnovsky never spoke about her experiences.

But she was clearly well educated in the German, French, and Russian languages, as well as her precise, British-accented English. And along with her dainty, colorful trademark—this morning it was a narrow length of glossy green satin—Carnovsky liked informal groupings. It's conducive to more intelligent involvement, she cheerily explained, as daily she had her class rearrange the rigid columns of tablet armchairs into a wide, open circle which encompassed the classroom, giving all students the chance to see each other clearly, and equally. In her large, mixed classes of black, white, and Hispanic students, Carnovsky was very strong on that word "equality."

Robyn noted, not without some fascination, the new vocabulary words which Carnovsky was writing on the blackboard for class to write in their notebooks:

Slothful	lazy, sluggish
Lethal	causing death, deadly
Lithe	bending easily, supple
Loathe	to feel disgust for, to hate
Soothe	to calm, to quiet, to comfort

Waving the green silk length to encourage a student to repeat the words after her, getting another to try more precise diction, asking this one and that to use the words in a sentence, Carnovsky was trying, as always, to inculcate good diction.

Robyn told herself ruefully, "I have been very slothful in my attendance." She gazed across the talkative circle to where Victor sat with some football friends. He sent back a smile and mouthed the words: "*Lithe*, that's you, kiddo!"

"Now since you're my brightest class," Carnovsky said crisply, receiving some yelps of approval for that pleasant observation, "and since most of you are getting ready to graduate, we're going to discuss a particular social value. Think about it. Here it is: What is the one thing, above all, you would like to do before you die? So you can say, my life has been worth living?"

That stopped the murmurous conversations cold.

Carnovsky had typically touched a chord in her students, and after a moment, she asked, "All right, who wants to begin?"

"You, Barbara?" someone called out.

A large, black girl seemed to know her mind, as she said unhesitatingly, "What interests me most is success. Success in the business world, that's for me. That's my game of life."

This was met with approving nods, and some groans. The girl Barbara held her ground—"And my mother and father like that idea, too"—as students freely commented. Robyn saw Victor and his friends talking it over.

A white boy said, "I want to go to law school and be a cop. That's my bag!"

Carnovsky stood calmly aside, listening to some applause and some derision: "A fuzz! Why?"

"Ever since I was ten, that's what I always wanted to be. My brother's a cop! My sister's a cop!"

"Oh, well, that's different!"

His neighbor, a slender Hispanic girl, put in, "I want to be a secretary, and get me a house, and move down South. I don't want my son to live in New York. There's not so much crime in the South. You can go out of your house and not think you'll be robbed while you're out." At sixteen, she was already the mother of a six-month-old baby.

Another black girl, looking stolidly at the young mother, said very quietly, "Me, I just want to be recognized. That will make my life worth living."

"Recognized for what?"

"Just . . . *recognized.*" She fell silent, declining to amplify further.

For the next half hour, Carnovsky stood on the sideline, letting her students take over, occasionally moving the question along so that all could participate.

"I want to be an architect—leave my mark on the world by leaving buildings all over the place."

"I'd like to be a singer or a model. I'm sure I can make it."

"The only way I can see to really achieve something is to get into politics. World politics, I mean. Be in power to change things!"

"I want to do some work to help the world get peace; make it a place where people live together as friends."

"I want to be a pro football player . . ." (Someone chortled, "I knew someone would have to say that!")

A tall, attractive boy said calmly, "I just want to be rich!"

This broke up the class, and someone shouted merrily, "On the day you're going to die?"

Carnovsky cooled it. The reactions to her question continued to be lively, but still very personal. Robyn wondered about the drift. The students were talking about what they wanted to be or have; but wasn't Carnovsky trying to get them to stretch their minds more, beyond material possessions?

When it was her turn, Robyn said, "I want to see the world! Everything in the world! Paris, Venice, London, Moscow—Africa, China! I want to see what people live in those places, and how they live. Everything we've been studying in school—I want to see it all come to life!"

"That's a very big order," someone near Victor drawled.

"I *need* to see it," she insisted, "because I want to write, and I want to be an actress, a *good* actress. I believe I can't be that unless I educate myself liberally in life. I have this powerful curiosity about all people!"

"Aren't you going to need money to do all that?" asked the boy who wanted to be rich.

This earned him another yell of laughter.

It was nearly bell time before Victor spoke up. He spoke with confidence, and, it seemed to Robyn, mostly to her though he didn't single her out by look or deed. His words fell on the class precisely, with diction almost as faultless as Carnovsky's. He seemed to be judging, at least obliquely, the others' windows on the future, while trying to illumine his own, something intensely personal.

"This *is* a game of life—I like that phrase," he said. "The real game is just beginning for us. We're young. We have it in our power to make the game work, if not miracles, perhaps some wonders. I think Miss Carnovsky expected us to be more philosophical, and not so materialistic or self-centered. To think on—even daydream on—what we want to do *that matters*, that will make a difference to us and to the world, before we die."

Robyn saw Carnovsky nodding vigorously in Victor's direction.

He went on, "Since we haven't real power in our hands yet, we can let our minds run riot; consider what we would do—maybe can do—if and when we get the power. Some of us will get it. For me . . ." He measured his words more. "I am going to be a doctor, probably a surgeon. I want to find cures for diseases. But mostly I want to study cause and effect; and that means planning my life in terms of research—medical, scientific, and human. Meaning not only on the body but also on the mind. Why? I like the idea of probing deep."

He stuck his glasses on top of his head, and continued, almost abstractly now, "I hope it doesn't remain an idea, that's all. I'd like it to be my life work. Because I expect it will force me to do another important thing: that is, *extend myself*. I mean, with people. With people's problems. All of us have to *extend* ourselves one way or another— to make it a really interesting 'game of life,' don't you think?"

Victor's speech was the longest, and when he finished, there was a stunning silence. Then, without any signal, the class burst into spontaneous applause. Carnovsky looked around beaming, as the bell rang for a change of class. Not all had applauded, however. As Robyn rose, she heard someone mutter cynically, "Thus saith the great Victor." And another said, "Nice, and very pompous, *don't you think*?" Her friend snickered.

But Robyn had been deeply stirred. She found herself wondering, who was Victor really challenging? Himself? Her? Robert, whom he'd asked to meet? Society?

She waved warmly to him as he headed for his next class which they did not share; he nodded back agreeably enough, but his expression seemed withdrawn, despite the applause. She felt a stab of confusion, finding herself at odds with her own questioning. Just how much, really, was he prepared to "extend" himself, say, with her father? True, he seemed ready enough, had asked to go with her to visit Robert. And she was the one who had hesitated, out of deference to her father's problems. But wasn't the hesitation also because she felt unsure—unsure of Victor's attitude? Was his speech some kind of self-analysis?

"That's traitorous," she scolded herself. "You heard. He believes in extending oneself. He said we all must."

Miss Carnovsky was motioning to her, with the lovely green silk thing, and Robyn hoped she could make her favorite teacher understand.

"I want to apologize for cutting class," said Robyn. "I'll make the work up this weekend. My term paper is half done."

"Fine. What I'm mostly concerned with is this note from you." Carnovsky was holding Robyn's letter. She let it drop on her ring binder containing the script of *The Crucible*, the coming school play. Robyn stared at her letter miserably.

"I can't do Abby at this time," she stammered.

"Why at *this* time?"

"I'm having problems."

"With the part?"

"With too many things."

"Personal things, you mean?"

"Kind of."

"Then they're not theatrical? I'd want to know about those, that is, if you're serious about acting."

"Oh, don't say that! You know I'm serious about acting."

"Then, what is it, Robyn?"

"It's . . . complex. Do you think . . . I was hoping you'd let me do one of the other parts, not Abby."

"A good actress, Robyn," Carnovsky said evenly, "does not tell a director what to do."

"I'm sorry."

"For heaven's sake, stop saying you're sorry! Listen to me: I cast you for Abby by deliberately casting against type. She's a mean, vicious, heartless, frightened person—who destroys what she can't have. It's a great part!"

"It is."

"You agree?"

"Oh, yes."

"And you can do it?"

"I know every line!"

"But?"

Robyn looked at Carnovsky, her eyes glittering with tears. "But I can't do Abby just now. I *loathe* her. I have such strong feelings against her. I don't want to let you down . . ."

"Your *self* down, Robyn."

"Okay, myself. I have too many problems right now."

"Want to talk about them?"

"I can't."

"Maybe I could help you."

"No. Thank you."

The teacher hesitated, seeing the other's distress, then went on in a more relaxed tone, "Tell you what, Robyn. Let's put your letter aside. I'll rehearse the scenes around your part. Meantime, would you think very hard about what you're asking me to do? The world out there, my dear," she went on, "is a chaotic jungle, theatrically speaking. The actor has to use personality, style, voice, to bring that jungle on stage, and interpret it. Creatively! What I'm leading up to is this: you spoke about your powerful curiosity. Here's your opportunity to free it—to take hold of your problems, whatever they are, and see them in terms of other people's lives. Turn them around creatively."

Carnovsky ran her fingers several times through the length of silk as she spoke, as though reliving some remarkable moment in her own private life. Robyn watched the affectionate strokes, almost feeling them on herself. "Let go, Robyn—whatever's troubling you," she said quietly. "You'll think things over?"

"I will, Miss Carnovsky."

"Good. Now,"—crisply the English teacher once more—"let's talk about your term paper."

Victor was waiting for her in the publications office. You look very jaunty, Robyn thought, in your leather bush jacket and the white fisherman's sweater.

"You were fantastic!" she greeted him.

"Oh, that thing in Carnovsky's gig." He sounded offhand, but obviously pleased.

Robyn laughed. "You know very well in her 'gig.' "

"Every word was for you."

"For us?" she prompted.

"Right."

"I'm seeing Daddy this weekend. He's asked to meet you now."

"So you've told him about me?"

"Of course."

"Oh, great."

Victor's reaction was hearty and prompt. So why did it make her feel uneasy? She couldn't help seeing again the withdrawn look he had worn in class, despite his splendid words.

You're imagining things, she told herself.

It's not as though he's just calling on Ethel and George. Daddy is different. And Victor's never met a . . . murderer. Say it! Murderer.

Oh, Lord, stop making problems . . .

Victor was scattering her thoughts: "You haven't forgotten, we're playing touch football on Saturday?"

"Forget! Who, me?"

She loved those afternoons together. Once a month, a dozen classmates drove in the Burnside station wagon to Van Cortlandt Park in the Bronx, to team girls against boys for an hour or two in the strenuous, improvised game of fun and strategy. They played almost without rules or goals, running and tackling one another, rough-and-tumble without the usual protective equipment. No side ever "won," but the girls teased the boys with their boast that "we're the better players!" The boys liked to keep it that way.

Some generally went horseback riding after the game. Then in the late afternoon, happy and spent with exertions, they would sit around on the grass, relaxing or talking or napping. It was always a grand time. And after the drive back to Manhattan, some would take in a movie or concert before going home.

But after the game this time . . .

Robyn said, "We can go on to meet Daddy afterwards. At Frank's Coffee House, near where he lives. He said we could meet there, if you like."

"Fine with me," he said.

10.

She had begun to anticipate the tensions at home, to dread most of all the new "silent treatment" she was getting from her mother. Perhaps George had asked Ethel to stay cool. A peaceable man who recoiled from scenes, he transferred to his club chair the moment dinner was over, to the television set, his evening paper, "his quiet time," as he jokingly called it, lighting up his pipe like a calumet of peace.

It was Ethel, quite erect these days, pale and tight-lipped, who symbolized the threatening atmosphere at home.

What on earth does Mom think is going to happen? Robyn thought desperately, as she and Joyce brought in the food platters from the kitchen, set them on the table, and joined their parents. Ethel's evening meals were always served quite formally on immaculate cloths, adorned with a centerpiece of flowers; on Sundays and holidays, the antique silver candelabra, a wedding gift from their employer, got the table's place of honor.

Why can't she see my side? Why can't she ever unbend?

And why does she act as if my seeing Daddy means it's the end of the world for us?

Mom, I do love you, but I do have a mind of my own! And a heart, too. After all, I love Daddy, too. Doesn't he need someone to believe in him? Who else is there but me?

"I didn't go to rehearsal today," Robyn said, determined to try for some conversation. "Maybe I'll drop out of the play."

Joyce looked up briefly with interest through her dark-tinted glasses, then went on eating.

Ethel said nothing.

George said, "Why's that?"

"The part's too heavy."

He gazed at her quizzically. "It's an important role, isn't it? Didn't you tell me it was . . ."—he smiled in a fatherly way—"fantastic?"

She smiled back, grateful for his small joke. "It still is, George. But it's very heavy. And I have so many . . . things to think about. Like the term paper," she hurried on. "Anyway, Miss Carnovsky, the drama coach, has asked me to think it over."

"And you'll do that?"

"Yes."

Silence again. Unendurable silence, except for the sudden swish of water as Joyce filled her glass from the copper pitcher. Robyn watched the other's concentration on her small task, as if the spilling of a single drop might plunge them all into a darker mood. Joyce was playing it safe, and her quiet concentration made Robyn impulsively throw caution away.

She said, rather too loudly, "Joyce, a bunch of us are driving to Van Cortlandt Park on Saturday—to play some touch football, maybe go horseback riding. Want to come with us?"

George looked very pleased. Joyce's head came up. She replaced the pitcher carefully, and regarded Robyn for a long moment.

"Well, Joyce?" asked George.

"I'm thinking it over," Joyce drawled, miming Robyn's earlier words. Robyn flushed and gave a short laugh. Suddenly, the other joined in, and before they knew it, they were two giggling schoolgirls. (Much later, Robyn realized that Joyce's quip had broken the tension, deliberately.) Joyce finally said, "No, I can't go. I've begun waiting tables at the Three Brothers on Saturdays."

"They paying you union scale?"

"They'd just better!" Joyce retorted.

This earned another smile from George. And Ethel managed a small one. She still hadn't spoken to Robyn; and the girl thought, not without bitterness, okay, Mom, I can't help it, I have to tell you this, so here goes: "After the game, Victor and I are planning to meet my father. We won't stay long."

"That so?" George said. He ran his tongue over his lips, and his eyes sought Ethel's. Warningly, it seemed to Robyn. But her mother was quite controlled and rather prim as she broke her silence, and inquired acidly, "Why? Is Robert now some sort of celebrity?"

"Hey, that's good," said Joyce.

"Joyce!" warned George.

"Oh, Mother, please . . . !"

"Anyway, you're going to do it, so why tell us?"

"But Victor *asked* to meet him."

"Victor did?"

"I wanted you to know."

"Just that?"

"What do you mean, Mom?"

"I mean, you're not bothering to ask if we approve?"

"*Would* you, Mom?"

"No."

"That's why."

"And if, even now, if I told you—if *we* asked you—not to do this?"

"Please, Mom, don't."

"But, damn it, I *am* asking you!"

George got up then, shoving back his chair, and going quietly to his retreat. Robyn watched him go miserably, hoping for some generous witticism from him to break the tension; but he seemed as rigid as Ethel, with controlled anger. The silence that filled the rooms was pervasive.

She did not reply to her mother. And later, when she and Joyce did the cleaning up, the dreadful silence was like a wall between them again. George's moods always seemed to affect Joyce that way. Yet Robyn had glimpsed that other side of her again tonight.

For a moment . . . and now lost?

The playing field in the Bronx park was not as graceful a setting as that of the Sheep Meadow in Central Park. The latter was encircled twice over, first by the great arc of leafy trees, then by the skyscraper panorama of Manhattan itself. But neither was the Bronx setting as crowded as at Central Park, and the dozen boys and girls who had driven up with Victor and Robyn knew exactly where their favorite grassy islet lay. They were delighted to find it empty.

"It's freaky, the way it waits just for us!" someone shouted. Without ceremony, they dumped their duffel bags and books, and the girls squared off, not without some self-conscious laughter, against the boys.

They played for nearly an hour without a pause, before flopping down like exhausted, blue-jeaned birds on the cool grass, under an immensely spreading tree. The rough-and-tumble, friendly play, with lots and lots of running, was really, as Robyn characterized it, "just playing happy." Now they were happy enough to relax quietly with one another, under a shared tree.

After a while, they decided they were hungry. Several went off to buy hot dogs and Cokes, to be paid for out of their football pool.

Victor and Robyn lay close together.

Her hair fell in long tangles, damp from the perspiration, but she felt too marvelously lazy to brush it. The dampness made her yellow sweater cling tight. She squinted up at the cloudless blue sky with supreme contentedness. From the distance, she heard the multiple city noises with honkings of cars, an insistent police siren; but close up she felt the sweetness of nature, the birds hopping fearlessly near their prone figures, a squirrel daring to approach, a large, veined leaf floating down and resting on Victor's sweaty white T-shirt. Dreamily, she turned to her friend, raising herself on an elbow to gaze at him. He turned to face her.

"Good game?" he asked lazily.

"Fantastic!"

"But you've really got to learn to hold the ball properly," he said, his eyes gleaming with mischief, "right against you, here." And he reached over and cupped her breasts with both hands. His movement surprised her, and though she felt a rush of pleasure with his touch, she drew back involuntarily, smiling and self-conscious.

He gazed at her fondly. "I'm not looking to collect," he said, still sounding lazy.

She bent over then, and kissed him.

"You're just nice to touch," he said, as he closed his eyes.

She ran her hand over his brow and nose and mouth, and wished that the afternoon would never end.

The others returned with their lunches. They got up then and sat around and talked about the game, and all agreed, as usual, that "the girls are better than the boys!"

Three or four decided to go horseback riding with Victor and Robyn. They rode confidently, cantering when the sandy trails were wide enough for safety. And it seemed to Robyn, riding ahead of Victor, that this was one of the perfect times of her life.

It was close to five o'clock when the riders took their horses to the stable, and returned to their football friends. They piled into the station wagon. Victor took the scenic West Side Highway back to Manhattan, and the river traffic on the Hudson, which was glittering in the late afternoon sunshine, seemed to the contented girl to be "playing happy" too.

Victor dropped the others off on Riverside Drive. Then he and Robyn continued on alone to Frank's, near West Twenty-ninth Street. In the car, they donned their identical, heavy white fisherman's sweaters and brown suede vests. Robyn brushed her hair, gone thickly unruly, over each shoulder, wiped her face with a moist towelette, and applied some light makeup. Victor borrowed her compact to stare briefly at himself in the mirror; then he severely brushed his own tangled, bristly black hair. They prepared themselves automatically, as though unwilling to voice their sudden tension.

At last Victor asked, "What's he like?"

"You can relax," she said.

"No, honestly."

"Probably as nervous as we are right now."

"Think so?"

"I'm sure of it."

"What'll I call him?"

"Call him? Robert."

"Not Mr. Adam?"

She laughed. "Whatever's more comfortable for you."

Her father had reserved the booth near the door, and was waiting for them. Frank's was half empty at that early hour, and none of the others from the Center seemed to be present.

He kissed Robyn. "Hello, Robyn girl. Had a good day?"

"Wonderful. Daddy, this is Victor Burnside."

"How are you, Mr. Adam."

He took Victor's outstretched hand and began to shake it warmly. Then he dropped it and stared from one to the other in surprise. "Well, what d'ye know?" he exclaimed. "His-and-hers, in person! We used to joke about that in . . ." He broke off in embarrassment, his face tightening.

"Let's sit down," he said.

He recovered himself as they sat in the booth, and candidly addressing himself to Victor, he went on, "Like I said, inside we used to joke about it, only we called it his-and-*his*. Get it? You know about the prison, of course." He tried to make it casual, but it came out abrupt. Victor flushed.

"Yes, sir." Victor's response was polite, and her father nodded agreeably enough. It was Robyn who appeared shaken by Robert's awkward words, and Victor's distant response. The waitress appeared, pad in hand, for their orders.

"We had a late lunch," Victor said politely, "so all I want is coffee." Robyn nodded her agreement.

"Coffee for three then," her father told the waitress, and she jotted it down and went away.

"How old are you, Victor?"

"Seventeen, sir."

Robert gazed at him uneasily.

"Why lay on the 'sir'?"

"Sir? Oh, habit, I guess."

"Well, lad, we're not in school now. You can drop it."

"Sir?"

"Oh, come on!"

Victor's face fell, and he went very pale. "Mr. Adam, I say 'sir' even to my father."

"What is it with you two!" Robyn burst out.

"My fault; Robyn girl. I thought you were putting me on, lad," her father said quietly.

"No, *sir*."

"I'm a bit nervous, I guess. Meeting my daughter's best friend, you know."

"I understand."

Victor was looking straight into her father's eyes, as though taking his measure as surely as her father was taking Victor's. Her father went on, looking suddenly very old and gaunt, "You know, most people think ex-convicts are some kind of freaks."

The boy shrugged, and Robyn put in, "You mustn't be so sensitive, Daddy. Victor does understand."

The coffee came, and as they drank it, they each seemed to be waiting for the others to begin again. Her father said, "Had a good day then, Robyn?"

She began to tell him about it, and Victor smilingly threw in the old crack about the girls being better players than the boys, and that got them laughing. Robert asked whether city horses were really any good. And Victor, who had spent two summers on dude ranches, got into a pleasant discussion with him about the more lively, ranch-free horses. They were more relaxed now, but Robyn couldn't help contrasting her father with George Grenshaw at home, that stolid and humorous, straight father.

That's it, of course, she thought.

Daddy doesn't know how to play the straight father with a grown-up daughter. With a boyfriend.

He's been away so long . . .

He needs time to get used to me, to us.

Get rid of his fears.

Get rid of his suspicions.

Frank's place was filling up, and then without warning, the Stick stood at their table, gnomelike and all eyes, grabbing her father's hand, pumping it up and down.

"Hiya, Bob, hiya, girl, everybody! Geez! You're a treat for sore eyes! I'm back in the Center, Bob. Johnny kept his word, you know!"

"I know."

"Never gonna get busted again."

"Okay, okay."

"I'm clean now, Bob."

"Stop it with the Bob!"

"Gonna stay clean, that's the only way, right? That's the truth, ain't it?"

"Clear off, Stick, I'm busy."

"Can I have some coffee with ya?"

"No!"

"It's just that . . ."

"Goddammit, get lost, will you?"

Her father half rose from his seat in a terrible rage. Olaf the Stick fell back as though bruised by it. He stared around the booth; then like a whipped dog he scuttled away. Her father sank down, and he seemed to crumple, his faded eyes unable to meet theirs.

"He's such a pest," he muttered.

"Also a dope addict, isn't he?" Victor asked evenly.

"He says he's clean. You heard."

"Victor's planning to study medicine, Daddy," Robyn

put in hurriedly. "His father's a doctor, and he's going into research."

"That right?" But her father seemed drained, withdrawn, hardly aware of the boy's affirmative answer. When he looked at them again, he said sadly, "It was a mistake to bring you here. Robyn girl, find another place for us next time. Look here, Victor," he went on in a monotone now, "most of the people here have done time, like me; or are out on parole. I don't want her here. But when we meet again, in a different place, we'll really take time to know each other." He forced a smile. "Have a proper meal, and I'll pay from my own salary. Not depend on the Center."

"That's it!" said Robyn. "We haven't even talked about your job. How is it going?"

"Next time, love."

"Okay, Daddy. It's just that . . ."

"Next time, Victor?" he asked the boy directly.

"Certainly, sir."

Robert winced on that, as he stood up, virtually dismissing them. Robyn caught her father's reaction, and wondered, too, at the boy's edgy tone.

"Thanks for coming. Gotta be going now."

"I'll phone you, Daddy."

"You do that, love."

They took their time walking to the Burnsides' station wagon, each full of thoughts. Robyn, reacting to the other's querulous mood, said at last, "What's bothering you, Victor?"

"I'm not sure."

"Was it my father?"

"That's some place," he said, evasively.

"Was it my father?"

"Anyway, a hangout for dope fiends, isn't it?"

"You wanted to meet him."

"I'm glad I did. He's . . . interesting."

"My God! You mean, like a specimen?"

"Now who's being sensitive?"

"What is it, then?"

"I don't know."

"What *is* it? Say it!"

"Well, for one thing, you didn't get down to any real questions. And I couldn't."

"What questions?"

"The real nitty-gritty." He paused before saying clearly, "His crime. Why he did what he did."

"I don't know the answer . . . yet."

"But that's the whole point. Don't you want to have the facts?"

"Of course I want the facts," she cried. "I have a very deep curiosity about the facts—about that whole time of his life and my life! But you saw what happened to him in there!"

"What?"

"When that man, the Stick, came up! Daddy was embarrassed and humiliated. It was painful!"

"Oh, that."

"Yes, that! He was so hurt, so frightened."

The boy shrugged. "That's *his* problem."

"Only his?"

Her throat felt tight and dry, and she found she was resenting the other's hard, magisterial tone.

What's really bugging you, Victor? Didn't you mean a word of that great monologue about people extending themselves—involving themselves?

They got in the car, and as he put it in gear, she stared straight ahead, holding back her tears.

"It's not that I don't want to *extend* myself," he said suddenly, as though reading her thoughts. "But I need the facts to understand properly, and to make up my mind. Don't you agree, Robyn?"

"But this wasn't the time."

The sky, so cloudless and brightly blue a few hours ago, was becoming overcast. She couldn't bring herself to sit closer to Victor, to look at him. She struggled to see the episode realistically, from his point of view. She had been just as shocked as Robert when the Stick appeared and was so insistent, until her father seemed ready to punch him.

Oh, God, wasn't that the way he'd been *before* prison? So he still flew into those murderous rages? In that awful moment, he had looked as if he could have killed the Stick!

Stop dramatizing.

He was just humiliated on my account, and with Victor sitting there.

But why did Victor have to be so . . . so scrupulously polite, with his airs and his "sirs."

And why did Victor think they could—or should—get all the answers, all the "facts," in this first meeting?

"This wasn't the time," she repeated, more to herself than to Victor.

What, she thought, has happened to my perfect day?

11.

A contribution to *The Beacon,* in response to its publicity drive for stories, poetry, and art, lay on Robyn's desk in the publications office. It was carefully typed on good, white bond paper, reflecting the author's pride in work; and just above the author's name, address, and phone number, was its shocking, provocative title: "Paroled—But Am I Free?"

Robyn stared at the manuscript and the writer's name for some moments before turning the cover page to read. For it came from a girl whose court case had been a nine-day wonder in school: the senior, Shelley Clark.

Robyn knew the girl only in passing, among the school population of some three thousand students. But Clark was very well known publicly. Her imprisonment upstate, as a chronic runaway and youthful offender, and her case against the State of New York for "cruel and unusual punishment" while incarcerated in isolation, had been in all the newspapers. Now the girl was chiefly known as a loner and a grind. She appeared to spend most of her free time doing makeup work and in the library, and also tutoring.

"Deedee was my friend in the so-called training school," her short story began.

> *We knew each other for only a short time inside prison, but our experiences there and later, on the outside, locked us together in such love and such fear, that we were more, far more than friends in trouble. We became sisters. So when Deedee killed*

herself at an early age—sixteen—because she wouldn't let the State own her again and take her back to prison, part of me died with Deedee.

Deedee's story is sort of my story, too. Yet here I am, I'm safe, I'm alive. Technically, I'm free. But even after I come off parole, will I ever feel really free again?

Mesmerized now by the candid opening, written obviously for shock value, Robyn read on, dimly aware that Victor had come in and was sitting opposite her at their partner-desk. He busied himself. Once or twice when she looked up to acknowledge and nod to him, she found him staring at her thoughtfully.

The story was fiction, but Robyn was aware that only one who had personally suffered such episodes could write with such authority. She also realized that the story held her because of its parallel with her father's. Was this outpouring then an attempt at self-analysis? Was the girl still so insecure? For she wound up asking herself some punishing questions:

Deedee's dead but me—I'm supposed to be free, on parole, as they call it. I'm expected to really grow up and live free in the real world. But how free am I? How do I stop depriving myself of the oxygen I need for my soul—the oxygen called self-respect?

Whatever experiences were still haunting this girl were probably haunting her father, weren't they? She wondered if Clark could help her; advise her . . . She gazed at the manuscript, then across at Victor. She wanted to tell him that she felt curiously close to the author, wondering what impelled her to write so candidly for classmates, many of whom, she wrote, either feared or despised her. She had spirit: in her story she had called them "the no-no people."

But Robyn held in her reactions, wanting a detached view from Victor.

"I'd like your opinion of this story," she said.

"Well, I know what yours is," Victor said.

"You do!"

"I've been watching you."

She smiled fleetingly. "Well, since you're so psychic, see if you agree." She tossed the story to him.

He looked at the title, and gave a start. Without a word, he draped his long legs over the arm of his chair, and began Clark's story. Robyn left him to it. She went out and drank deeply at the water fountain in the corridor, but the girls in Clark's story went with her.

How alone they must have felt!

Like frightened animals. Trapped.

One died, one lived . . . with the Clark girl demanding to know: who was better off in a rejecting world?

But hadn't she found her answer? Otherwise, why was she here at school, working, tutoring, wanting. as she wrote, to be a writer, for she was named after a great one?

"I see why you're taken with the story," Victor said when she got back to the desk. Robyn eyed him calmly. Don't go psychological on me now, she thought; I know you're seeing the parallel, too . . . "But the story grabs you on its merits."

"Good! Let's lead the next issue with it," she said.

"I'm doubtful," he said, frowning.

"Why not?"

"Well, it is a graduation issue."

"All the more reason, don't you think? Give her some of that . . . oxygen. She's heading for college, like us."

"I was thinking of a great cartoon to lead the issue," he persisted.

"Listen, her whole life's been a cartoon!"

He shifted uneasily. "Well, if you feel that strongly."

"I do. I'd like to phone her the news."

"Do you have to?"

"If she's like me, she's on tenterhooks."

"She's not at all like you, for God's sake!" He got up

to stretch, and his back was to Robyn. "She's been on the street, on dope, a hustler. Some of the boys even . . ."

"Go on."

"Let's drop it."

"Why? Does it involve anyone I know?" she asked. "You?"

He hesitated a fraction before replying.

"Don't be funny."

"Anyway, what's it got to do with her writing?"

"Nothing."

"You know, I think I'll ask her to the house tonight. Have dinner with us," she said impetuously. She was provoked by their exchange.

He looked incredulous. "You mean that?"

"Why not? *Extend* myself. Talk over her story."

"And some other things?"

"Maybe. She's on parole, isn't she?" Robyn asked toughly. She was still bothered by his hesitation.

"That should make your parents hysterically happy, to know that."

"Sometimes, Victor Burnside, you act like an awful uptight square!"

"And you, kiddo—you are a realist?" He sounded rueful and worried. The crack sobered her, and she slowly replied, "I'm trying to be."

Ethel and George were used to having the girls' friends in. They encouraged it. They also liked to know in whose homes the girls visited, not for invidious reasons but because they believed in being "caring" parents. Victor was a regular caller, especially on weekends. And Joyce's friends sometimes stayed overnight, after a movie or concert. The Grenshaws prided themselves on their "open house" attitude.

In spite of tensions, Ethel was very gracious to Robyn's guest. It would be hard, anyway, to be otherwise with a girl like Shelley. She was a strikingly pretty blond, tall and slender like Robyn, her wide, hazel eyes taking in the pleasant apartment with candid appreciation.

"It's all so pretty here," she exclaimed after greeting Ethel and George. "Such warm colors everywhere. Lovely."

"Why, thank you," Ethel said.

"It's got such a warm, lived-in look! And all those books, and the piano. You've got practically a garden indoors with those great plants!"

Ethel was beaming. "In your home, too?"

Shelley laughed. "Oh, no. But we're trying. My mother—my foster mother, that is—has a real green thumb."

Ethel said, with a curious look, "Oh, really."

The two girls went to Robyn's room, Robyn explaining that they needed to talk over the other's contribution to *The Beacon.* Later at dinner, Ethel said, "Tell us about your story, Shelley."

For a moment, the girl seemed uncertain, looking for approval to Robyn. But Robyn sat silent, wanting the other to decide. The girl said, not a little shyly, "You see, I was named for the great poet, and one day I hope to write a book. So I thought my personal experiences could be a start, with a short story. I really flipped when Robyn phoned me the news."

"The news?"

"That's it's to lead the next issue!"

Ethel flashed her good hostess smile.

"Wonderful," said George.

"Must be terrific," Joyce said agreeably.

"It's very good," Robyn said. Adding, for effect, "Victor agrees with me."

"You see, it's based on my experiences in the State training schools," Shelley explained, quietly.

"That a fact," said George.

He was casual enough, but Robyn was aware that he didn't look at the girl and was holding his fork with immense care in the ensuing silence.

Ethel's smile was gone. She sat very erect and still, as she looked from Shelley to Robyn. But Joyce was all ears, leaning forward, adjusting her dark glasses, waiting to hear more.

"What's it called?" she asked.

" 'Paroled—But Am I Free?'—a question mark."

"Why the question mark?"

The girl's eyes darkened, and looked faraway. "I'm not sure why, actually. I guess it's because I don't really feel free yet. You know, free of the past."

"Why's that?"

"Well, maybe I imagine it, but I feel the kids don't trust me."

George said, not unkindly, "Obviously Robyn trusts you, Shelley, or you wouldn't be here."

"That's true!" she burst out, sending him such a radiant smile that he flushed. But his fatherly comment was lost on Ethel.

"You're with a foster family?" she asked dryly.

"I have a foster mother."

"Where's your own mother?"

The girl faltered. "She's . . . around."

"And do you see her?"

"No, no, never! She doesn't want me anyway."

"Do you want to tell us why?"

"Mother, please!" Robyn said.

"It's okay, Robyn," Shelley said, her eyes almost shuttered with some inner turmoil. "My mother's an alcoholic. And I'm afraid of her husband."

"Oh?"

"My foster mother's a wonder. She's old and jokes about being a human antique. But she saved my life. I love her." There was a sudden touch of defiance in Shelley's tone. She sat up very straight, the hazel eyes searching theirs, it seemed to Robyn, for some understanding.

"No generation gap," Joyce said.

"No *intelligence* gap," said Robyn, earnestly.

The girl sent them both a grateful look.

But Ethel shoved back her chair. She got up and said with cold control, "Would you excuse me, everyone? I have a headache."

"Mother, I'm sorry."

"Me, too," Ethel said pointedly.

"Victor's coming over later . . ."

"Give him my best," she snapped. She nodded to Shelley, and swept out of the room.

Robyn watched her mother go, in shock and growing anger. Her rude and utter rejection was unmistakable.

Mom, what's really happening to you—to us?

Okay, so I'm curious about Shelley.

But there are plenty of other kids in school who've been busted, and paid the price. Some of them are the *real* straights now.

Couldn't you see that we were just asking you to believe that people can change?

Robyn could hardly bear to look at Shelley, who had gone quite pale, and drooped as her mother swept out. George's head was down, and he was murmuring something polite, before retreating to his corner and pipe.

It was Joyce, the family maverick, who astonishingly saved the situation in her own unique way. She took off her glasses and rubbed her eyes, and looked straight at Shelley, said, "Well, I don't have a headache, and I do have something to say."

She avoided Robyn's hard and threatening look, and went on in a level tone, "You have to make it for yourself, don't you, Shelley? Some people will down you. I mean, some time people will bury you below, if you let them. But it's up to you to make it for yourself, I say. So you have to stay strong, don't you agree?"

Shelley nodded, mutely. But the color came back to her face.

Robyn said, in amazement, "That's cool, Joyce."

"What?"

"The way you put that. You really do understand."

"All you're telling me, you know, is that you . . . that some people can be really dumb-dumb," Joyce said airily, "about other people."

She tried to sound cool, but she put her dark-tinted

glasses back on so quickly that Robyn was sure she was hiding her own emotions.

Robyn said, "You're so right," as she contemplated the other for a long, satisfying moment.

12.

A light rain was falling as Robyn and Victor walked Shelley Clark home that evening—Victor very correct with the girl, while applauding her contribution—and dropping her off at her West Eighty-fourth Street brownstone house, not far from school.

The evening's dramatic climax made Robyn want to draw close to Victor, spill it all out, reach for his encouragement. But in some strange way, another part of her resisted the impulse. Ever since the meeting with her father, they'd had little time together, except for *The Beacon* conference on contributions. True, they were all under pressures with end-of-term exams coming, the prospect of college visits for those who were college-bound, the senior class play, the closing games of the season. But they'd been under similar pressures before and always managed to meet, go on drives, take walks, making a snug world of their own. They hadn't done any of that for days.

Now they walked along without touching. Automatically, they were continuing down to Riverside Drive, one of their favored walks, now oblivious of the weather, though Robyn did tie a bright, red, silk scarf on her head against the rain.

"That looks like one of Carnovsky's," Victor said.

"She gave it to me when I got the part of Abby. Wants me to use it in the forest scene."

"You're doing the part then?"

"I haven't decided."

"Won't you have to, pretty soon?"

93

"Yes."

She linked her arm with his. They walked this way in silence, and she was conscious of the way the rain misted the yellow street lamps and the gently swaying trees, and sent the ubiquitous pigeons swarming for shelter in the leafier ones. Until she could stand the oppressive silence no longer, and asked, "What is it, Victor?"

"I was wondering how it went—with your parents."

Robyn made a face.

"Mine, too," Victor said abruptly.

"What do you mean, yours, too?"

"They're . . . people are afraid of ex-cons."

She dropped her arm. "You told them about my father?"

"I had to, didn't I?"

"You promised it was between us," she stammered, "for the time being."

"Do you object to my father knowing about your father?" Victor demanded. She shivered with sudden cold.

"No, no, I guess not."

"I felt I had to tell him, Robyn."

"Okay."

Don't dramatize this now! He did what he thought was right. Though he broke his promise. But how easily he had slid into the hurtful jargon—ex-cons! Why not use the less punishing terms, like ex-offenders, or parolees? And what did he mean, people were afraid of ex-cons? Why was his father afraid for his son?

"How much did you tell him?" she asked.

"That we met, had coffee, saw his friends."

"Friends? You mean, the Stick?"

"That, too."

"And?"

"Frankly, he said he didn't like any of it. He said he didn't like that whole scene."

Robyn stopped, and shrugged off Victor's arm. She stared ahead, feeling the rejection personally somehow, as she said quietly, "Just like that."

"Well, what else could you expect?" Victor laughed uneasily. "He sees sick people all the time."

"What did you say then?"

He spun Robyn around until she faced him, and said, "I told him *Robyn's* my friend, not her father! I said the man's been in prison, now he's out and has a job, and he's trying to stay alive. Okay with you?"

She blinked back her tears.

"And my father said," he went on deliberately, "that's all very well, but the man's been a killer . . . no, don't pull away, you wanted to know, Robyn . . . the man's been a killer, and in one of his rages, he might kill again. Now, that's what he said."

She pulled away again.

"And you? What did you say?"

"I just walked away from him."

"You . . . just walked away."

"Without another word."

"So that's your idea," she cried angrily, "of extending yourself, is it? Just walking away!"

"What the hell," he retorted. "He's an old man of forty-five, and he's only known sick people all his life, so he probably thinks your father is infectious! Listen, I don't want to hurt him. So when he asked me to give up the whole scene . . ."

"Oh, yes, the *whole* scene!"

"That's the way he put it, I did the best thing at that moment and walked away."

"So what about us, Victor?"

"Us?"

"I'm in that 'whole scene' which he wants you to give up."

"He meant your father."

"You sure?"

"Don't be flaky, you freak!" he exclaimed. He pulled her to him, and kissed her fiercely. She clung to him, responding with all her strength.

"You've got to understand," he murmured, "that

people are afraid of ex-cons. They really are *afraid* of them!"

"Please! Stop saying that, Victor," she said.

But ironically, his words found an echo at home.

Ethel and George stood as one, waiting for her return, and they seemed as implacable as the wall which figured almost daily now in her fantasizing. For a mad moment, she wanted to crash the wall, rush into her mother's arms as she used to when she was little.

The moment passed.

She took off her wet kerchief and jacket, and said a tentative "Hi," and waited. This time, it was George who took the initiative, as though, the girl thought bitterly, he'd been elected.

"You upset your mother, bringing that girl here."

"What's wrong with *that* girl?"

"She's an ex-convict, isn't she?"

"Oh, Lord!"

"And just what does that mean, Robyn?"

"Oh, skip it."

"Well, isn't she?"

"She's not a criminal, George. Yes, she was in trouble, and yes, she's been in juvenile prison. But that's all in the past. She's not in trouble now. She's got a foster mother she adores. And she's written a fine story for our magazine. I just wanted to know her a bit better, outside of school. That's all there was to it. And by the way," she went on emphatically, "she told Victor and me that she's been accepted by Cornell University. She wants to teach, she says."

"Teach what? Morals?" Ethel put in acidly.

"Mom, you act as though people can't change!" Robyn cried.

George patted Ethel's arm as though cautioning her to stay calm.

"Well, you shouldn't be mixing with that lot," he went on. And with chagrin, Robyn could hear echoes of

Robert's similar words earlier on. "Anyway, not in this home. Not with Joyce here."

"Oh, George, you big old square," she said lightly. "Joyce is more grown up and mature than you give her credit for. I know."

For an instant, George looked very pleased. "I hope so."

Ethel said firmly, "Get on with it, George."

He looked from mother to daughter. "Shelley did say she was on parole, didn't she?"

"Is that what you're uptight about?"

"We have to know if that's why you brought her here ... to show us an example or something."

"What do you mean, George?" Robyn was stalling.

"So you could, uh, demonstrate to us someone who's been in prison, who's on parole. Now, was that in your mind?"

"What difference can it make? I'm curious about her. Yes, her being a parolee had something to do with it. But her writing really interests me, too. I wanted to get to know her. You'll notice she doesn't have horns growing from her head," she added ironically.

"Don't you be talking that way to George!" Ethel said harshly. "You managed it very cleverly. And that's the reason for this talk."

"Oh? You call this *talking*, Mom?"

Ethel bit her lip.

The old sickness of fear and confusion was pinching Robyn's stomach again, and in the dreadful pause which followed her bitter comment, she found herself wishing that the maverick of the family was here, if only to stick in some small malicious or mischievous joke. But Joyce was nowhere to be seen; probably banished to her room during the confrontation. George was twisting his empty pipe, and trying to mask his own uneasiness.

He went on carefully, "We really do love you, Robyn. You know that. So at the risk of being called not only a big, old square but a big, old, old-fashioned square, we're asking you not to continue your relationship with this girl

. . ." He hesitated a fraction. " . . . or with Robert Adam. In other words, Robyn, ex-convicts are absolutely to be avoided. Now, your mother and I agree, those are the rules. People have to live by certain boundaries and rules, and those are ours."

Robyn's gaze went from him to her mother and back to George. She was really drawn to this man. He was kind and good, and she felt that the harsh edict was being spelled out so clearly for her because it was his way of keeping peace. Peace as he and Ethel saw it. They had the power, of course, to do this: it was their marriage, their home. Their way of showing they cared.

But it couldn't be her way. She didn't want to be in their power—not on this question of being Robert Adam's daughter.

"And I love you both and respect your feelings," she said at last, "but I can't accept your rules. I'm just hoping that in time you can respect the way *I* feel, too. I don't know how all this is going to work—your feeling one way and me another. But my father needs my help." She saw her mother flinch, and felt a bit self-conscious herself at the dramatic-sounding words. But she desperately wanted them to see Robert as she saw him.

"He's a frightened man right now. He has no one else to turn to who really cares about him. I have to do what I think is right, here at home and . . . and in life. I feel that. Maybe I act by intuition, by what my heart tells me instead of my head, but is that bad? I'm sorry you don't like it. But, won't you try to see it my way sometime?"

Ethel said sharply, "You keep dramatizing everything! His needs for you!" She rushed on, angry and contemptuous. "Well, it's crazy! You'll drag us all into another terrible agony again. I know it!"

"What agony? How?"

"I'm sure of it!"

Her mother's face, usually composed and youthful-looking, seemed contorted, so hard-eyed had it gone.

"Either you abide by our rules, as George has put it," she said, "or else."

"Or else what, Mom? Or else I'm not welcome in this family?"

"You're seventeen now. You're not a child, You figure that out!"

13.

At the Center, Johnny greeted her with mild surprise.

"I thought you knew, Robyn. Your father moved out."

She stammered, "Daddy and I have been out of touch for a few days."

"Well, everything seems fine with him," Johnny reassured her at once. "It was that, as you know, he didn't feel free here, and I can understand the feeling. He found a place close by. Wait here a minute."

A couple of the men, pausing in their game of pool, threw her an eager smile and an appraising look. She smiled back vaguely, speculating that not many people came visiting; she wished she felt easy enough to approach them, talk to them. She had a sudden feeling that that was perhaps what they most wanted: someone to talk to.

There you go again, dramatizing, she scolded herself.

Victor's right . . .

Mom's right . . .

Concentrate on Daddy. He's number-one priority.

Johnny was back with a slip of paper.

"As you see, he's close by," he said.

Robyn stared in fascination at the address, for it was on the historic, landmark street with the ivied gardens which they'd admired on Robert's first evening back in New York.

"He loves that street, Johnny," she said.

She found the dignified three-story brownstone house, set well back from the pavement. A low, wrought-iron gate opened to a garden carpeted with ivy which had also fingered its way up to the top floor.

"A picture-book house," she murmured happily as she rang the bell on the mailbox bearing Robert's name.

"It's me!"

"Robyn girl, come on up."

The buzzer released the front door, and Robert's great shout of welcome from up above seemed to lend wings to her feet. He hugged her close.

"My first visitor to my castle!"

"Oh, Daddy, like old times."

The Victorian house indeed seemed like a fortress of privacy. The apartment with its high-beamed ceiling ran the width of what had been a parlor, now converted into the living room with a fireplace. Behind a tall screen was a tiny, well-equipped kitchen. Opening at one end of the living room was a bedroom, which faced the red-brick wall of the high-rise apartment house just beyond. Robert grimaced as he showed Robyn the wall.

"That's the one drawback," he said. "But the shades can be kept drawn all the time there."

She said lightly, "It's not a real wall—just another house. This place is fantastic, Daddy. You got lucky."

"It's Johnny," Robert said. "He's got the people on this block involved in the work of the Center. He says they're his 'helpers.' "

"That Johnny!"

"Can you stay a while, Robyn?"

"Yes."

"I've been saving a bag of chocolate-chip cookies and ice cream for you."

"So you knew I'd come!"

"Of course."

Robyn was to remember later that, above all in the hours that followed, they were comfortable together—really comfortable—for the first time since she was small. Here in a place he could call his own home, her father already looked different: the faded blue eyes in his gaunt face were not so abstracted as they talked; and in appearance, in the pair of old jeans and tieless shirt, sleeves rolled above the elbows, he reflected some new self-assurance.

Until he talked about his job.

"Well, a couple of the old-timers there do make me nervous. They seem to know about my record. They can be sarcastic at times."

"Like what?"

"It's hard to put your finger on it, but to them I'm some sort of branded animal. No, it's true, Robyn . . ." as she began to protest. "For instance, one of them cracked, 'You don't want to mess with that dude, Jamie. I hear he stuck up Wells Fargo. Oh, sorry, that was last night's TV. Just what was it again, Adam?' "

"Big joke," Robyn said miserably. "What do you do when they act up?"

"Try to ignore it."

"Of course."

"It's not easy, Robyn. I'm human. I start to feel angry, I'm not denying." His voice had gone flinty, and his mouth tightened in a way that Robyn had come to fear. "Know what my boss's secretary did just yesterday? She had to leak out that my P.O. had been in to see the boss. Now practically everyone in the place knows I'm on parole."

"But does the P.O. have to put himself on view? Couldn't he have phoned, been more discreet?"

"A lot of P.O.'s are good fellows, and handle their investigations that way. But not mine, Robyn. Not mine."

"So he's proved you're on the job. I hope he's satisfied. Now you can forget it."

"Maybe." But then his face cleared and the old infectious smile lit his eyes. "But you know, two of the new employees, hadn't been there long, actually came over to me and made a real thing out of trying to be helpful. And one said, in a very loud voice, 'You're doing a great job.' Decent fellow."

"He was just being human, Daddy."

Robert wanted to take her out to dinner, to celebrate.

But Robyn said no, she wasn't hungry, she wanted to talk, "get to know each other again." He agreed, but he did a surprising thing. He went to the chest of drawers, and from the bottom drawer he withdrew a pint-sized bottle of bourbon. It was half-empty.

Robyn stared. "Should you be. . . ?"

"D'you know how long I've had this little bottle?" he put in quickly. "A whole week. I don't drink, Robyn, believe me. It's only for once in a while."

"But even that's dangerous, isn't it?"

"Not by the thimbleful, like this and in my own home."

He poured a small amount of bourbon into an empty coffee cup, and, with eyes half-closed as though in pleasant expectation, he tipped back his head and took the drink straight. He slapped the cork in the bottle and shoved it back in the bottom drawer. "That's all I need, just once in a while. See, I'm not being a phony . . . I wanted you to know."

There was a pause. She watched him put the kettle on for coffee, then, sucking in her breath, she decided to take the plunge. "Daddy?"

"Yes?"

"Since you're levelling with me, I need to know . . . I have to understand what you did in Grandma's house, and why you did it."

He went on making the coffee. He poured them two cups, and sat down opposite Robyn at the round oak table. He stirred his instant black coffee slowly as he stared at his daughter. The faded blue eyes seemed as pale and unblinking as a blind man's. "You're asking, how did I come to kill him?"

"Yes."

"But that's all in the past, isn't it, Robyn? It's done with, and I've paid for it."

"But I've never known what really happened. I need to know, Daddy."

"That's important to you?"

"It's not healthy to keep thinking about it, is it? Not knowing why it happened?"

"Not healthy for whom?"

"Well, for me."

He drank his coffee. "To be honest, Robyn," he said at last, "for me, too, I think."

She wanted him to understand her motive: "It's just that I feel I need to see the whole picture of my life, and not in the bits and pieces that I half remember. The bits don't fit together, Daddy, and I don't want to exaggerate them in my mind. I've only a vague memory, for instance, of my grandmother who's back in Ireland now. But I do remember that I loved her very much."

"And . . . her husband?"

"Him, too."

She saw he was beginning to sweat. Perspiration appeared in the deep furrows of his forehead and some trickled down his temples into his eyes. She was suddenly aware that he was trembling, the way he used to tremble in the old days after a drinking bout. And something inside her wanted to cry out to him, protectively, but also out of some old dread, "Never mind, forget what I asked." But he spoke first as he stood up and drained his coffee cup.

He said, "You above all have a right to know."

14.

Robert's faded eyes were shuttered with some driving fear as he struggled to find the way and the words for his daughter. "If I don't tell it now, it will only get harder, won't it? And you, Robyn girl, must be feeling like a pawn on the old chessboard which everyone is pushing around. I can't have that, can I?"

He went on, "What is true, Robyn, is that I killed a man. Of course I'm desperately sorry about that. I didn't even know at the time that I'd killed him, you know, but that doesn't lessen the enormity of the crime. I happened to hate him. And I was drunk, stoned out of my skull, when I did it."

"I saw that reported in the newspapers."

"You never came to the trial?"

"No. Mom thought it best to keep me away."

"She was right."

He lit a cigarette. Robyn saw his eyes stray to the chest of drawers where he'd put the bottle, but instead he drew himself up and poured himself more coffee. "You know what's an interesting sidelight that I could never puzzle out, with all my supposed intelligence. The long sentence. After all, I'd been killing men I didn't even know or hate in the war in Vietnam, and was actually decorated for doing that. Here for a single crazy act of self-defense, I was being imprisoned for killing a man who'd been hurting another." She caught the self-mockery in his tone.

"Self-defense? You'd been fighting?"

"Fist-fighting. Maybe I threw the first punch, maybe he did, I was too drunk to remember . . ." Adam wiped his

105

brow, and went to stand at the window which overlooked the tree-shaded street. He turned back to Robyn abruptly. "Why the hell am I lying to you? Sure I hit him first. I must have. I went over there with the idea of beating him up. He'd been beating my mother. Christ, I couldn't let that go on. I suppose I was saying to myself I'll kill the bugger if he doesn't stop, something like that."

"You were thinking like that?"

"Who knows?" He stared at her with his blind man's stare again. "I suppose—it's six years ago now—I didn't have a clear thought about that, Robyn. I was so drunk, with anger in my soul and not only the liquor. But, well, 'didn't mean to do it, your honor' is no defense, girl. Anyway, there must have been *some* premeditation in it. God, I've spent enough years behind bars mulling that one over. There was one man in the slammer, a counselor, whom I saw a couple of times whom I could talk to . . . about this violence I've got in me . . . it's *there*, Robyn."

He paused again. When he spoke, the tone was very level, no longer trying to justify his actions. "The real truth that I can face now is that I was jealous. How can that be, you might ask? I'm not a stupid man. I'm somewhat educated. I love books and poetry and music. But in one way, I loved too much, too . . . possessively, which means neurotically. That's the part of me that never matured, I guess . . . the relationship with my mother."

She realized that he was adrift on his own feelings and memories now, and she sat quietly listening, going with his mood. In the developing dusk, he seemed unable or unwilling to put on the lights, and she was unwilling to break the mood. So they sat now at table, close together, letting the mood have its way, in some almost mystical family rapport. Robyn was aware that her father was using her as a kind of sounding board for his feelings. But she also felt that this was as much a catharsis for her, too.

He went on, "There were times when I actually was behaving as though I was her husband instead of her son. I realize that now. But we were alone, and for most of my life I think we were very protective of each other. She'd worked so hard for me. I loved her for that, and, well, dammit, I felt even after I married your mother that I remained closest to my mother. And I'm sure she, in turn, bound me close to her. We never had secrets from each other, and she could bash me one when I needed that, too."

He broke off with a chuckle. "I remember when a couple of kids and me—we were about fifteen—we helped ourselves to some motorcycles in Central Park. We didn't think of it as stealing, we just wanted a joyride, didn't want to hurt anyone, you understand. Well, the cops caught up with us, took us to the precinct station and called our parents. We were let off with a warning and probation. But my mother was so scandalized—no, disgusted—with the episode that she kept me indoors after school for weeks. 'I'll not be having these criminals anywhere near you!' she kept saying, even though I told her I had been the ringleader. She never believed that. We Irish stick together, you know—she'd protect me no matter what! Same way as I felt about her! That is," he took a deep breath, "until she shacked up with that bloody sadist ... young enough to be her son, he was!"

"Shacked up? Daddy, they were married!"

"So?"

He got up then and put the lights on. He stared with his abstract, unseeing eyes again at Robyn. He was far in the past. "He was trying to take my place with my mother because I'd married and left home. Well, that's what I thought, what I felt. He was never good enough for her. And he *beat* her. That much I knew for sure."

Robyn was remembering, too, the abrasive arguments on that question. "But Mom used to say that Grandma loved him anyway."

"How could she love that sadist?"

He turned away again, but he had a compulsion to continue reliving the past: "That particular night is not too clear in my mind, Robyn. I guess I'd been boiling over for a long time, over the way he treated her. I felt I'd have to do something about it. At the same time, everything was

going wrong on my job and at home. I'd been goofing off
on the job . . . drinking, Robyn, drinking hard because I
hated the work, feeling frustrated about my whole useless
existence. That night, I think I must have developed the
idea that my mother's husband, my stepfather, was responsible for all my troubles. Don't forget it was a pretty
drunken head, Robyn."

He rubbed his eyes, as if to rub away the pictures they
must be seeing again. When he looked at Robyn, the eyes
had grown hard, and his mouth a tight line of control. "It
wasn't much of a fight. Mom was somewhere in her
kitchen when it began, and I remember he yelled something like 'Don't show up drunk in *my* house,' and he
raised his hand toward me—but when I hit him he wasn't
ready for it, and he fell back. I kept hitting him, and he
landed one or two. But I had the upper hand. And, that
was it. When he fell the last time, his head must have hit
the radiator. Meantime, Mom had come in yelling at both
of us. After he went down, Mom was bending over him
and shouting at me to get out and never come back. I
didn't know he was dead till I read it in the papers."

The silence that now hung over the room was unbear-
able. Robyn, shaken and drained, said, "I had to hear it
from you yourself, Daddy. You understand."

"It's all right."

"I still have to know something."

"What?"

"When you learned you'd killed him, how did you feel?
I have to know."

"My God!" he said. "What sort of a question . . .
okay, I can tell you. Maybe it was a mixed feeling at first,
that my mother was rid of such scum. But when I got
really sober, I knew what a terrible thing I had done. I'd
ruined my life in a way I'd never thought possible. And
wrecked it for everyone I loved. You, Ethel, Mom. So I'll
have that to live with always. But I've paid for it, haven't
I? And now I can make it back somehow, with just a little
help. But I know I can't make it alone."

Robyn crossed to him then, and they held each other for a minute. Tight.

When she spoke, it was to tell him the truth of her own situation. "I'm forbidden to go on seeing you. But I have to do what I think is right, Daddy, and that means that I can't live by their rules at home. So they've indicated— Ethel and George—that they don't want me at home. They don't want to get involved in any way."

"Good God, Robyn, what am I doing to you?"

"I've thought about it. I though we could meet secretly . . ."

"Yes. Let it be that way."

She shook her head. "No . . . it wouldn't work. I'd have to be lying to them all the time. I love them too much for that."

"What will you do then?"

"Leave home."

"Oh, no. Not that."

"It'll be all right, if you let me come here."

"Here?"

He held her at arm's length and studied her intently. She saw his eyes fill with tears and the color flood his face. "You really mean that, Robyn girl?"

She was aware of the longing in his voice.

"I haven't thought it through yet. I'll need a few days to make the change. But if you want me . . ."

"Want you! I'll make the bedroom into your own studio, just for you and your friends."

"That would be great."

"I'll do everything to make you happy. We'll be a family, you and I."

"Fantastic!"

"If it's really what you want, Robyn."

"It is. We've both had enough of rejection and fear."

"Then it was worth it," he said, his face glowing with relief, "I mean, getting that old story out in the open, once and for all. I was so afraid."

"We can help each other," she said in a fiercely protective tone.

"Ah, I hope so, Robyn."

He gave her a key to the apartment.

"Did I tell you, Daddy," she said, "that I'm taking back your name—Adam?"

15.

She told Victor in the publications office about her long session with Robert, and her decision. The boy gazed at her in shock and disbelief. At first, he tried a small joke.

"I think your parents and some others would call that plan a no-no," he said.

"And what do *you* call it, since I'm about to be thrown out?" she asked quietly.

"A no-no. In fact, it's insane."

"That's it?"

"You can't be serious."

"It's only for a few months. Till graduation. I'm sure to enroll for a summer course upstate."

"What about us?"

"Us?"

"Where'll we meet?"

"In my new home—in Daddy's apartment. If you like."

"No way."

There was a silence. She went on, "Well, it's a big city out there, Victor. We can meet anywhere you like. Your place?"

"What about how my parents feel?"

"What about it?"

"But I've told you."

"Listen, are we really talking about *us*, Victor?"

"Of course."

"I wasn't sure."

"What's that supposed to mean?"

"I had the distinct feeling we were talking again about your father and his reactions."

"I suppose we are, in a way."

"I thought you believed in extending yourself."

"To what? Your insane plot?"

"You think I'm just dramatizing things again?"

"Well, aren't you, Robyn?"

"Dammit, I've told you—either I stop seeing my father, or else leave home. Now that's the choice."

"Well, frankly, I agree with your mother."

"You do. Well, put yourself in my place. Would *you* stop seeing your father?"

"My father would never have done such a . . . criminal thing."

"Why? Don't doctors ever kill? Bad surgery, or something like that?"

"It's not the same thing."

"Okay. But all I'm trying to reach you with is that all kinds of people can get caught in some terrible, revolting thing, and have to pay for it. But do we go on rejecting and rejecting them, after they've been punished?"

"You think that's what this argument is about, Robyn?"

"To me it is."

"Well, to me it seems that you're the real rejector," he snapped. "You're the one rejecting your true parents and your home. You're the one rejecting my feelings. You're even the one rejecting your commitment to the school play—to the drama department. And you're the one rejecting our . . . our mutual ideals."

"How's that again?"

"You keep dramatizing the situation when it's perfectly clear," he went on, as though lecturing his lessers. "My father says Robert Adam made his bed and let him lie on it, but not drag you into it with him." He saw her flinch at the clumsy metaphor. It seemed to bother Victor too, for he went on in a small voice, "What he meant was, stop trying to be to him what he was to *his* mother."

"Is that what you think I'm doing, Victor?"

"No. I just think you're going on impulses. I don't want to hurt you . . ."

"*But.* There is a but?"

"Yes, dammit. But . . . I don't want to get involved with . . . with Robert Adam. Not if it means you're actually going to live with him."

"I asked you to put yourself in my place."

"I can't . . . it couldn't happen to *my* father, that's all," he said, looking like a granite-stern stranger again.

He picked up his books. They were both stunned by the sharp exchange, and didn't touch. He sent her a nod and a murmured "see you later," and started out. She nodded back mechanically in reply.

For the next few days, she concentrated on her term paper, one deadline which had to be met before making her move to her father's apartment. And she stayed longer hours at school, working also on the last issue of *The Beacon* which still needed some art work and proofreading. She worked mostly alone on the issue, Victor sending her an excuse (by note) that he was needed in his father's laboratory the rest of that week.

She refused to dwell on what really lay behind his excuse, concentrating on the last issue of her high-school career as an editor, and, to her surprise, rather relishing the decision-making process which was suddenly her own.

Shelley Clark stopped by now and then. They bought Cokes and talked about their college plans. Acting on an impulse, Robyn told Shelley that her father was also out on parole. The other eyed her thoughtfully. "That can be tough, Robyn."

"Tough for whom?"

"Why, for him. I guess he's finding out that people can be afraid of ex-cons."

"I'm trying to help him."

"Okay, but you have to be careful, too."

"What does that mean?"

"Well, a lot of people may be watching him, you know. Parole officers, other ex-cons, waiting for him to 'take a fall,' violate his parole, something like that, which lands him back in prison. If you're seen with him, you'll go into his official file, you know."

"His P.O. knows me already."

"Well, just make sure your father sticks with the parole rules."

Robyn said, "I expect he will. He must."

Shelley shifted in her chair uncomfortably. "It's quite a list, those parole rules, Robyn. I think you should get him to go over them with you."

"Thanks. I will."

At home, she managed to stay close to her room, avoiding her parents and Joyce and their unspoken questions. In any case, Ethel had reverted to the "silent treatment"; and George, despite his patient smiles, seemed to be all for that as he retreated nightly to his television corner and pipe. She had not told them of her decision, and the very quiet in the house seemed more threatening than confrontations, as she tried to still her mixed emotions of grief and guilt.

Meantime, she devoted herself to the term paper. She had elected to define social and political values in life; in fact, she felt that her instructor had obliquely given her the title—"A Celebration of Values."

"When it comes to considering social justice," the teacher had said, "questions of mutual trust are also involved. So try to see life as a celebration of values—*your* particular values. For instance, examine such terms as freedom and social justice carefully. They're so noble sounding, aren't they? Only they can mean different things to different people—to some, anarchy; to others, social conflict. Try for a perspective that's your own. Because tragedy, as one old philosopher liked to put it, is the conflict of *right with right*."

Wasn't that the tragedy here, too, at home?

Wasn't it a "conflict of right with right"?

They had right on their side.

But so did she!

And wasn't Robert Adam reaching for his "right"?

Even Victor had his "right"—his own?

She had chosen the road she would follow.

Was she cruelly dividing the family, as Victor seemed to imply? Or were they the ones on an obsolete road, unwilling to come even partway with her along her chosen road?

It occurred to her, as she struggled to return her attention to the term paper and her notes for it, that ironically there might be one member of the family who understood her choice: Joyce, the maverick.

But at the moment, for her own private reasons, Joyce was keeping her distance with the others.

16.

On Friday of that week, she left with a suitcase of clothes, her tape recorder, and her typewriter, before Ethel and George got home from work. She had seen Joyce in school, and told her of her plan to live with Robert for the time being.

Once more she was touched by the other's reaction.

Joyce had stammered, "Stay strong, Robyn," and given her an awkward hug.

Now before leaving, Robyn gazed around the quiet orderly apartment, which had been home since her mother's marriage to George, with a strange feeling of loss. As though each article of furniture and wall decoration and plant was already going out of focus in her mind's eye. She stood the envelope containing her note on the piano's music rack. She knew every word in it:

> *Dearest Mom and dearest George,*
> *I'm going to live with my father for the time being, because I don't want to have to lie to you, and I'd have to if I went on seeing him. I would want to see him, if I lived here. Who else can he turn to for help? He needs me, and I need him, too. I can't go on being split in two this way. So I'll keep in touch. I love you both very much.*
>
> *Robyn Adam*

She got a taxi to her father's address. She suddenly realized that Victor, who usually telephoned her on Fridays or routinely dropped in to take her for a drive or to a show and plan for the next park outing, wouldn't know where to reach her. She hoped he'd telephone the Center; Johnny would put him right. But would Victor do that?

He'd said he'd "see her later" last time they'd met. That had been days ago, after they'd scrapped. They hadn't really talked since then.

Were they also at breaking point?

She let herself into her father's apartment and, to her pleasant surprise, saw that he'd already shifted things around in anticipation of her coming.

The big, overstuffed couch was shoved against a far wall near the bookshelves; and a tall, moveable screen nearby could shield that sleeping area from the rest of the living room. On the table near the tiny kitchen, he had arranged dinner things on place mats, and stuck a small pink crocus plant in the middle for a centerpiece. She stared at the bedroom, now literally a studio for her, with a daybed, a colorful shaggy rug and small desk with brass handles. He had even taped a greeting to the top of the desk. It pictured a robin playing on a violin while it sang —"Everything's coming up shamrocks!"

So Irish it made her laugh.

Her head throbbed with the day's confusion. She went to the refrigerator and got a Coke. It was relatively early, and she thought, "I'll just lie down a bit before unpacking," and slipped off her shoes and lay down on the daybed. She pulled the fluffy green blanket up to her chin. A couple of hours later, when Robert arrived, he found her so deeply asleep that he decided not to wake her.

Resolutely, he did not go to the bottom drawer of his bureau, but, retiring to his own corner, he dozed off himself. It was the telephone, ringing obstinately, which brought them both to their feet.

Robyn heard her father answering it in low tones, apparently trying not to disturb her. But she went to him as he talked, and kissed him and he smiled at her while he finished the conversation.

As he hung up he exclaimed, "How do you like what I've done, Robyn?"

"Fantastic!" they both said together with a laugh.

"Why didn't you wake me?" she demanded.

"You looked so tired."

"Who was it on the phone?"

"You expecting a call?"

"I thought . . . maybe Victor . . ."

"Does he have the number?"

"Well, no. I guess not."

"It was just a friend of mine."

She looked so disappointed that he said impulsively, "Robyn, let's go out for dinner. What do you say?"

"With all that food in the refrigerator!"

"Never mind. It's a red-letter evening for me!"

Another kind of letter was probably being opened at that very moment by Ethel or George, she thought, the pain stabbing her temples again. She made herself ignore it.

Later, when Robyn reflected on her new life with Robert, it seemed odd how quickly one can adjust when pushed to it. She felt quite grown up as she now kept house for her father, listened to his confidences about his job and fellow workers, and his hopes. Johnny hired her to do some typing and filing a few hours a week at the Center, which paid for her carfare and school lunches. Indeed, Johnny continued to be their strong right arm supporting Robert's return "to the world."

"The first couple of months on the outside are always the hardest for these men," Johnny told her. "Especially for those who've been intimidated by loss of family and friends. Institutionalized people have terrible difficulty adjusting to the streets again. They're thrown into a fast-moving life where they have to relearn survival, start making their own decisions, and being men again, not numbers. So they depend to a big extent on their P.O.'s."

"Daddy seems to hate his P.O., Johnny. And it seems to be mutual."

The big man shifted his weight from one foot to another. as he said noncommitally, "Tough. Robert has his conditions of parole. He has to learn to abide by them, Robyn. Do you know that more than half of all prisoners released are thrown back in prison for one reason or other?"

"Violation of parole?"

"Yes."

She remembered Shelley's warning, too, and one night after dinner Robyn brought up the question of parole conditions bluntly. "Did they give you a paper to sign, Daddy when you got parole?"

"Damn right they did. All spelled out." He sounded bitter.

"Maybe I should know what's expected. Okay?"

"Sure. Why not? You have a right to know."

He kept his private papers in a heavy brown envelope in the top drawer of his bureau. Now he drew from it several sheets. headed "State of New York, Department of Correctional Services. Certificate of Release On Parole." His name, prison and conviction details, and date of release from Green Haven Prison were neatly typed above the rules and restrictions which parolees must agree to. She read on:

I, __Robert Michael Adam, GrH-13457__ , in consideration of being granted release, promise, with full knowledge that failure to keep such promise may result in the revocation of my release, that I will faithfully keep all the conditions specified in this agreement and all other conditions and instructions given to me by the Board or any of its representatives.

1. I will proceed directly to __314 W. 40th St., N.Y., N.Y.__ , the place to which I have been released (spending funds only for necessities), and within twenty-four hours, I will make my arrival report to

__Mr. Mortimer Locke__

NYS Dept. of Corr. Services (Parole) .

2. I will not leave the State of New York or any other State to which I may be released or transferred, or any area as defined by the Parole

Officer, without the written or documented permission of my Parole Officer.

3. (a) I will fully comply with the instructions of my Parole Officer. (b) I will make office and written reports as I am directed. (c) I will reply promptly, fully and truthfully, to my communication from a Member of the Board, a Parole Officer, or other authorized representative of the Board. (d) I am aware that making false reports may be considered a violation of the condition of my release.

4. (a) I will permit my Parole Officer to visit me at my residence or place of employment. (b) I will discuss with my Parole Officer any proposed changes in my residence, and I will not change my residence without prior approval of my Parole Officer. (c) I understand that I am legally in the custody of the Department and that my person, residence, or any property under my control may be searched by my Parole Officer or by any other representative of the Board. (d) If so directed, I will observe a curfew.

5. I will avoid the excessive use of alcohol beverages. If so directed by the Parole Board or my Parole Officer, I will abstain completely from the use of alcoholic beverages.

6. (a) I will make every effort to secure and maintain gainful employment. (b) If, for any reason, I lose my employment, I will report this to my Parole Officer immediately and I will cooperate fully in finding new employment. (c) I will not voluntarily quit my employment without prior approval of my Parole Officer.

7. (a) I will lead a law-abiding life and conduct myself as a good citizen. (b) I will not knowingly be in the company of or fraternize with any person having a criminal record. If there are unavoidable circumstances (such as work, school, family or group therapy and the like), I will discuss these with my Parole Officer and seek his permission. (c) I will support my dependents, if any, and assume toward them my legal and moral obligations. (d) I promise my behavior will not be a menace to the safety or well-being of myself, other individuals, or to society. (e) I will advise my Parole Officer at any time that I am questioned or arrested by members of any law enforcement agency.

8. I will consult with my Parole Officer before applying for a license to marry.

9. I will not carry from the correctional institution from which I am released, or cause to be delivered or sent to any correctional institution any written or verbal message or any object or property of any kind without proper permission.

10. (a) Upon my release, I will advise my Parole Officer as to the status of any driver's license I possess. (b) I will seek and obtain permission of my Parole Officer before applying for or renewing a driver's license. (c) I will request and obtain permission of my Parole Officer before owning or purchasing any motor vehicle.

11. I will not own, possess, or purchase firearms or weapons of any kind.

12. I will not use, possess, or purchase any illegal drugs or use or possess those that have been unlawfully obtained.

13. Should the occasion arise, I will waive extradition and will not resist being returned to the State of New York.

(Signed) _Robert Michael Adam_

She said quietly, handing the papers back to him, "I just wanted to know exactly what you're up against."

She saw him sag as though under terrible pressure as he nodded and replaced the documents. "I can't help feeling rotten that I'm making you part of all this now."

"It was my own decision, Daddy."

"With a little help from me," he said ironically.

"Oh, come on," she chided, "we're family, aren't we?"

"That we are, love."

"Listen, I didn't know you had a middle name . . . Michael! I learned something today."

He looked at her thoughtfully, with a twisted smile. "Darlin', we were reserving it for the brother you were to have someday."

17.

She telephoned her mother, and it was a coldly controlled Ethel who responded when she said, "You know I don't want to hurt you, Mom."

"You have and you will."

"But it was the only thing to do. I miss you, Mom."

"Take care of yourself."

"Don't you want my address and phone number?"

"No."

"I thought maybe . . ."

"We don't want to know where he is or what he's doing," Ethel said quite evenly. "I can reach you at school, if I need to."

"If that's the way you want it, Mom, okay. Give George my regards."

In a way, it was what she might have expected from her mother. But Victor was the real and terrible enigma.

He refused to bend. Though they still sat opposite each other in Carnovsky's class, and worked in the close quarters in the publications office, he seemed very far from her. He worked rapidly, barely looked her way, left with a distant and polite "see you later."

But there was no "later."

He asked no questions about her life with her father, nor how to reach her there. Finally, just before leaving work on *The Beacon* one day, she said casually, "Is the game on for this Saturday, Victor?"

Though the tone was light, she felt something shadowy and afraid within her; and she fidgeted with the papers on her desk waiting for his reaction, and started to tie Carnovsky's red silk scarf around her head, leaving streamers dangling behind. When he gazed at her coldly, she continued in a harder tone, "Well? Touch football. Should I tell the others?"

"I'm working pretty hard in my father's lab these days," he said evasively.

"On Saturdays?"

"Yes."

"Oh? Sundays, too?"

"I will be."

"Sure that's the reason?"

"Dead sure."

"Know what I miss, Victor?" she said, trying to keep her rising anger down.

"What?"

"Your *'kiddo.'* You didn't say, dead sure *'kiddo.'* Well, I miss that."

"Oh, yes?"

"It used to have such a nice, intimate sound . . . know what I mean?"

He said coldly, "Now that you mention it, I would be stupid to use it on someone with a . . . savior complex."

"Oh, of course. Could never be stupid."

"I don't want to quarrel with you."

"We have to talk."

"What about?"

"Us."

"I haven't the time."

"You haven't . . . kiddo?" she said, the sarcasm concealing her real fears. She placed herself in front of him, forcing him to stop gazing at the legends on the wall and look at her. She wanted desperately to touch him, but at the same time she drew back at the naked anger she saw reflected in his dark eyes. She tried again, softly now.

"Don't you want to know where I'm living, whether you can help?"

"How can I help?"

"Every way."

"I can't do that. Though I have given it a lot of thought."

"Why can't you help?"

"Because you've chosen to go and live with an ex-convict, a killer."

"But dammit, he's my father! I have to help him."

"It's the wrong way for you to help him."

"But if not me . . . who?" she cried.

"There you go with the savior complex. He's got to make it back on his own. He's got to do it himself, or it won't work. But no one's saying you shouldn't see him once in a while."

"My parents did. They forbade me *ever* to see him again."

"So that's the way the ball has to fall then."

"That old cliché! How about if we grab the ball and carry it for a change, and hold on to it, in spite of the others coming at us?"

The shaft had gone home, and she could see she had hurt him deeply. He tried to turn from her gaze, but she caught his arm. "I'm not finished, Victor."

He pulled away roughly. "I am."

She gazed at him then with a sad and searching look. "You really mean that, don't you?"

He didn't reply immediately. He looked unhappy and confused and Robyn waited. After a moment, he said, "I guess I do."

"Okay."

She took his school ring off the middle finger of her right hand, and placed it carefully on the desk. "I guess it was about time," she said, "that we really got to know each other."

Then she picked up some manuscripts, and her books, and walking rapidly, the streamers of the crimson silk scarf floating behind her, she left. Her tears came as she walked away, with only her pride to sustain her.

How's that for an exit, Carnovsky?

I think you'd have approved.

I think you'd have said that at least I did that with style.

18.

Above the daybed in Robyn's studio, Robert had hung a large, antique map of Dublin, which he'd found in a Greenwich Village bookshop, and framed for her "as an heirloom," he said whimsically. It was a multicolored map with bright green, not unexpectedly, dominating; and lettered boldly across the top was the original name for Eire's capital city—*Atha Cliath*. The Gaelic term, Robert explained, stood for "ford of the hurdles," to commemorate how an ancient king, trying to get home, had to hurdle many floods which had beset him.

At a point called St. Stephen's Green, Robert had stuck a small, passport-type picture of his mother. Clearly, the old map held more than symbolic interest.

"She loved to walk across the Green," he told Robyn, "and taste the salt wind blowing across the hedges and waterfall. On a sunny day, she'd go from there to the great courtyard of Dublin Castle, or to Trinity College park, a very decent walk. You and I will go to Dublin, one day," he went on quietly. "After all these years, she'll have forgiven me, don't you think, Robyn girl?"

"She will have," Robyn agreed.

In her heart, she wondered. Grandma had cut herself off so completely from the American branch of her family that she had not written to her son in prison, nor acknowledged Ethel's new marriage, nor replied to Robyn's letters. Yet Grandma couldn't have stopped loving *her*. When she was about twelve, a teddy bear with shiny, button-black eyes had arrived from Dublin, with a picture postcard of children fishing in the River Liffey—like an invitation, it seemed, to Robyn. But after that, silence.

One day she would visit Grandma in Dublin.

She had her roots there, too.

But the dated map made her shudder a bit: it was a skeleton out of the past.

One shouldn't be thinking about old hurdles and problems.

The present was the only thing.

Unconsciously, as she stared at the map and Grandma's picture, she took up the inflated leather football. She was turning it round and round in her hands, almost caressing it; as she became aware of her action, she gave a short laugh and tossed the ball into a far corner.

Enough of that—don't be flaky, she chided herself.

She turned to her homework, and was concentrating on the rest of her term paper, when the telephone rang. All at once her resolves faded. She ran to the phone, praying, Let it be Victor! Oh, God, let it be Victor, please!

But when she answered, she heard a woman's voice, querulous and demanding.

"Wanna talk to Bobby! Get Bobby on the phone!"

The woman's words were slurred.

"Bobby?"

"Wassa matter with you? This Bobby Adam's phone, ain't it?"

Robyn could hear a clinking of ice cubes in a glass at the other end, and an old sickness twisted her stomach. "Who is this, please?"

"Wanna talk to Bobby."

"Mr. Robert Adam is not at home," Robyn said.

The other mimicked. "Mr. Robert Adam . . ."

"Who is this?" Robyn stammered.

The demanding voice changed and got giggly. "Just tell him that Mimi phoned an' tell him I wanta see him tonight, even if he *has* lost his job. Tonight. Got it?"

"What's that? What did you say?"

But the woman had hung up.

Robyn made herself some tea. Could it be true? Dreadful memories began to flood her mind. She tried to shake them off as she drank the strong, hot cup of tea: the fights with Ethel because of his drinking; the way Ethel would clean out the whole apartment to work off her fears; the terrible telephone calls. Still dazed by the woman's drunken announcement, Robyn tried to go back to her homework. But it was no use.

She put on the radio and mechanically began to prepare the supper meal, and waited for her father. She felt frightened and inadequate, but, above all, angry that some strange, drunken woman knew something about his job and had his confidence more than she—Robyn—had.

It was quite late when finally her father arrived. He gave her a smile and a kiss. Robyn could smell liquor on his breath.

"Sorry to be late, but it's been rough today."

"So you stopped off for a drink."

"Aw, couple of beers never hurt anyone."

"That where you met Mimi?" she asked. He looked reproachful.

"Mimi? She been bothering you?"

"Daddy, you're not supposed to use alcohol."

"Now you're wrong, Robyn girl. It says, 'avoid excessive use.' Well, I do." And he sent another glum look her way, then went to wash up. It was not until they had finished supper, with Robert complimenting her on the baked ham and potatoes, that Robyn said in a worried tone. "This Mimi woman telephoned here, and she sounded drunk."

"Probably was."

"Who is she, Daddy?"

"Nobody."

"She called you Bobby. She said you'd lost your job."

His face was expressionless. He wiped his mouth with his napkin, and stood up. "Sounds like you two had a mighty interesting conversation."

"She did all the talking."

"She ask who you were?"

"I didn't tell her."

"Good."

There was a silence in the little apartment as Robert went looking for his cigarettes and an ashtray. Robyn hadn't stirred.

"I'll find another job. Don't worry, Robyn girl."

"What happened?"

The faded eyes looked bitter, and he looked suddenly very old. "It's hard to believe, and yet it's typical enough for an ex-con." He saw her flinch at the term, and he said wearily, "Just accept it. Everyone else does." The self-pitying note in his voice told her that he was turning inward again, as he went on: "The office was ripped off during the past weekend, or so it seemed. Someone had taken all the money out of the petty cash, about two hundred dollars which the boss keeps on hand to take clients out. The police were called in, and yours truly became the prime suspect."

"Daddy, no!"

"Someone told them I was an ex-con. So they called my P.O. and he showed up, too. The humiliation was quite complete, thank you," he said dryly.

"But you told them you were innocent, didn't you?"

His face was very pale, and he inhaled deeply. "I was the prime suspect, just out of prison, and so on. They had nothing else to go on. Even the boss didn't back me up. Let the cops take me to the precinct station, and in minutes they had a print-out on my record. It was a nightmare, and I saw that goddamn wall rearing up again."

"Well, you're here. They found the thief?"

He laughed harshly. "There wasn't any. The boss's wife had to go to Connecticut, and found herself short and knew about the petty cash box; she'd simply let herself into the office and borrowed the money. She forgot to tell him about it until she phoned her husband, and by that time I'd been held in the precinct pen."

"But where was your P.O.?"

"He *told* them to hold me while he was investigating where I'd spent my time."

"I can't believe it!"

"Believe it. He didn't even apologize when they let me out. Said I should expect it as 'routine' for as long as I'm on parole. Routine! What's routine about tearing a man's self-respect to pieces?"

"Oh, my God!"

"I went back to the office and picked up my things."

"You quit then?"

He said very quietly, "How could I stay there, Robyn? I'd always be under suspicion. The boss did call me into his office, tried to laugh it off, you know. Had a bottle of gin on his desk, and said he wanted to welcome me back with a drink. I didn't say a word. I just took the bottle and poured the gin all over his head."

"You *didn't*!"

"And when I walked out of that office, I felt much better."

"The P.O. will hear about *that*."

"Let him!"

"Johnny will help you find another job."

"I hope so."

"About that woman, Mimi . . ."

"What about her?"

"Well, she said you were to phone her. Tonight. Who is she. Daddy?"

"Forget it, Robyn. She's just someone I met in a bar. Like I said . . . nobody."

Johnny found Robert a job with a car wash not far from the Center. It was seasonal work which paid the minimum wage, two-fifty an hour, but at least it meant instant reemployment which was important for parole reasons.

At first Robert, depressed at the prospect of washing and vacuuming cars, was for holding out for "less demeaning" work; until Mortimer Locke, his P.O., started berating him on the phone for quitting his job "without prior approval." He lectured Robert about line six-c of the parole regulations: "I will not voluntarily quit my employment without prior approval of my Parole Officer . . ." and when Robert tried to justify his leaving the former job because of the unwarranted arrest, Locke went on berating him not only for quitting without permission from him, but also for his "violent action" against the boss.

"Lucky for you he's not pressing charges," Locke shouted at Robert over the telephone.

Robert replied, "I'm lucky all right."

"What's that mean, Adam?"

"Nothing."

"You better get yourself another job fast, man."

"I've got one."

He gave Locke the details.

Later Robert told his daughter grimly, "I've sure drawn a sickie with this P.O. He likes the power, he likes to see men grovel. He kept saying again, 'I'm in control of your life, man,' and why didn't I get his permission to quit. I managed to ask him flat out, 'You going to report me to your supervisor?' He said no, not yet. All that means is that he's storing up the technicals—violations that aren't real crimes—so he can go in with a whole list of parole violations that may land me back in the slammer."

"Well, you're not going to accommodate him!" she cried.

"Damn right."

"So you'll take this car-wash job."

"I must."

But her heart sank at the look in her father's face. The eyes were very pale and hard, unseeing, like those of a blind man.

19.

The past weeks had wrought a change in Robyn and it showed. She wasn't eating well, and had lost weight. The new tensions showed in her face, and the way that the light seemed to hurt her eyes. The partings from those she loved had been harder than she realized. All too often while someone was talking to her, she felt quite alone on some strange plateau of emotions. She found the tears starting without warning, as she tried desperately to sort out the problems in her new life.

For one thing, the woman, Mimi, now phoned Robert in a drunken haze two or three times a week, the mocking tone grown arrogant and possessive. Robyn only knew her voice, but she shrank from her imagery of the woman as she took down her messages for Robert, or heard Robert on the phone with her. Curiously, he seemed as depressed by the calls as Robyn was; yet he was obviously continuing to meet the woman though not in their apartment.

And Robyn was doing something that she despised herself for. When her father left for work, she would go to the bottom drawer of his bureau to check on the bottle which he kept there. It was clear that he was drinking again, and even before work. Moreover, he no longer bothered to conceal the bottles. As if grown careless about it? Or as if he knew Robyn was spying on him?

Well, that's what you're doing, isn't it—spying?

You hated it when Mom went through your things, and read your letters.

Now you're into the same dirty game.

But if he should keep on violating his parole . . . ?

Suppose he reported to that P.O. with liquor on his breath?

She felt a sense of danger all around her.

She was deep into the self-probing as she hurried through the noisy corridor crowds when Joyce's voice reached her, bell clear: "Hi, Robyn, where's the fire?"

She looked around, and saw Joyce waving to her near the school's inner courtyard. Robyn came out of her reverie and pushed her way across to Joyce.

"You looked real gone."

"I'm all right, Joyce. How are you? Don't you have a class?"

"It's prettier out here. Come on."

Robyn hesitated. She had cut too many classes lately, and now wanted to get to Carnovsky's and tell her that she had finally decided about the school play. But suddenly Joyce, with those staring, dark-tinted glasses and sloppy sweater hanging too big and loose over her jeans, looked unaccountably dear and familiar, and she wanted to be with her for a moment. She followed the other through the French doors into the courtyard.

Yes, it was pretty out there, and Robyn felt some of her desperation subside amid the green surroundings and serenity. Most of the students seemed to forget this was their property too, or had little time for it, since the majority had after-school jobs. But she and Victor would often work on *The Beacon* issues out here. The inner courtyard had been designed to look like a small classical amphitheatre, with Aztec-type sculptures adorning the stone walks. The forsythia bushes were already in bloom near the mimosa tree. And the other trees, tall maples coming into leaf, traced an arch, like some witchery, over the stony elevation which was used for a stage.

School festivals and plays were held here in the open, weather permitting; and more than ever, Robyn reflected, this natural setting was "made" for the coming production of a play like *The Crucible*.

Joyce, flopping down on a bench with her books hugged to her breast, brought a smile to Robyn's face for the other also seemed to be "made" for the surroundings, like an impudent pixie. She joined her stepsister.

"You're too thin," Joyce said.

"No, I'm okay."

"Listen, I won't beat about the bush. When are you coming to see us?"

"What?"

"I think you should come soon."

A sudden dread stabbed Robyn. "Is Mom ill?"

"Nobody's ill. But yes, in a funny way, you might say we all are."

"What does that mean?"

"I don't know. But something's gone wrong in the house, Robyn. Since you left, Ethel cries a lot. I know she worries about you all the time."

"She did what she thought was right, I guess," Robyn said in a flat tone.

"Well, she's had time to think it over. I hope so. Anyway, we don't talk about it. But Daddy . . . even he's quieter than usual, if that's possible."

"I'm sorry. You know I love George, too."

"I guess."

"But Mom said . . ."

"I know what she said, and what Dad said!" Joyce cried. "Forget it! Robyn, why don't you just take the initiative, drop in some evening. Like tonight."

"I could get thrown out again."

"You could."

Joyce was looking straight ahead, the sunlight glinting on her dark glasses. Her face was a tight mask, and Robyn found herself longing to take the enormous glasses off and see right into her sister's face.

The moment passed, and instead she said, very quietly, "All right, I'll come."

"Make it tonight. I'm waiting on tables tomorrow."

"Will you tell them?"

The other girl wavered. "No."

They fell silent. Sitting there, not touching, each into

her own thoughts, Robyn felt with a rising wonder that they were somehow closer than they'd ever been.

"I've got to get to Carnovsky's class," she said.

"I'll stay. Do my study period here. Listen . . . thanks."

When Robyn got to class, Carnovsky was deep into the school play, asking the students to explore the structure and values of it. As she talked, the teacher stroked a lovely, long length of yellow silk, the color of the forsythia bush near which Joyce now sat studying. And Robyn found herself thinking, like a child again with her crayon book, "Color this day yellow."

For Springtime? For new hope?

As she crossed to her seat, she dropped a prepared note on Victor's armrest. It told him of the staff meeting of *The Beacon* later that afternoon, hoped he could attend, "since it is the graduation issue." Later, she tried to catch his eyes, looking for some sign of interest; but he avoided that, and the rebuff was plain. He left immediately after class.

Robyn remained until all but Carnovsky had gone. The teacher gazed at her thoughtfully. "You've decided, haven't you?" Her grey eyes had lost their intensity, and twinkled at Robyn. "Let me guess: 'The play's the thing.'"

"Yes. I feel I'm ready, really ready now, to do the part of Abby, if you'll let me."

"Why, Robyn?"

"You may not like my reason."

"Try me."

"Well, there have been so many problems in my life lately, and I feel puzzled and angry a lot of the time, and, well, what I mean is, I feel a fusion with the girl Abby, because of all my problems."

"That's your reason?"

"That. And I've read the play over and over, and I can use the challenge. I can!"

Carnovsky said in a level voice, "I'm very glad you've

decided to come along with us, Robyn. But there's probably a far better and simpler reason why you should do Abby."

The girl waited, hoping that the vital, dynamic little woman with her world experience could in some way unravel the gone-crazy skein of her emotions. Carnovsky stroked the yellow silk length. "Simply put, it's because this is a good part for a good actress. Period."

Robyn gave a short laugh and gathered up her books. "Miss Carnovsky," she said, "thanks for cutting me down to size."

"Now, don't you be so ready to agree with me," the teacher said mildly. "You can act best when the head is cool and the heart is warm. I can guess," she went on, "at some of your problems—and that Victor, the genius, is one, yes? Well, any time you think I can help, remember . . ."

"I'll remember."

"Good. Ready for rehearsal now?"

"Yes. Yes, I'm ready."

20.

Rehearsal left her more exhilarated than she'd felt for weeks. The ungrudging acceptance of her back in the major role of Abby by everyone in cast and crew gave her the emotional edge she sought: enough control to push her private torments into the wings. Or use them to realize her role.

The Puritan girl, Abigail, according to the script, was "seventeen, a strikingly beautiful girl, an orphan; with an endless capacity for dissembling, however." That about summed up her mood, she told herself—feeling beautiful and damned. For she could not rub out the memory of the bottle in the bureau drawer; nor the rejection and slight by Victor, who had meant so much. She worked to fuse her mood with that of the beautiful Abby, as she cried:

> *"Uncle, the rumor of witchcraft is all about; I think you'd best go down and deny it yourself. The parlor's packed with people, sir. . . !"*

Rehearsal over, and the staff meeting of *The Beacon* begun, the exhilaration soon wore off. In the publications cubicle, she discussed drawings and space with the art editor, and began copyreading some last-minute poems. Shelley Clark had come, in response to an invitation; and her silky blond hair made a nice contrast with the high Afro of the black artist who was illustrating her story. Her cheeks flushed with excitement, exclaiming "That's super!" Robyn's mood was far from super. Victor had not shown up.

Why on earth had she expected him to?

She timed her visit to the Grenshaws so as to arrive after their dinner. It was George himself, pipe in hand, who opened the door, stared at her briefly, then hugged her affectionately.

"Ethel, look who's here!" he boomed.

He kept his arm around Robyn as he drew her into the living room. Ethel had started to rise from her chair, but she froze on seeing it was Robyn. Then she did a strange thing: she sank back into the chair and very quietly she began to cry.

"Oh, Mom, don't!"

"I'll be all right."

"Don't cry, Mom."

"I said I'll be all right."

"I wanted to come before."

George said, "Now put your books down. Here, I'll take them. We'll have some coffee."

"I don't know if you . . . if Mom . . ."

Ethel dried her eyes with her dainty, lace-trimmed handkerchief. "Why've you come, Robyn?"

"Why? I've wanted to see you. All of you. I miss you."

When Ethel didn't reply, George put in. "And we've missed you. We've all missed you, Robyn."

Joyce came from her room. Robyn speculated that the other had waited, with unaccustomed tact, until the preliminaries were over. Joyce said casually, "Hi, there. Want something to eat?"

"Hi. Everyone wants to feed me."

Ethel said pointedly, "Are you planning to stay?"

"I wish . . . you know why I can't, Mom."

"Well, then, I think . . ." her mother began. But George cut her off. He held his pipe before him, like a baton, and said quite firmly, "Coffee all round, okay? Joyce, please?"

"Come on, Robyn. Make yourself useful, too."

In the kitchen, the girls could hear their parents talking, then arguing, Ethel's voice sounding tearful. Robyn said, "She's frightened. It's not going to work, Joyce."

"It's working a bit already. You're here."

"She can't forgive, and she can't forget."

"Be patient."

Robyn said, "That, from you!"

"What do you mean?"

The high words in the other room were now falling on the apartment like sharp pebbles.

"Just that there have been times when I thought you hated having my mother and me here," Robyn said.

Joyce looked at her, while placing the mugs of coffee on the tray very carefully, as though mulling that one over. Then she adjusted her glasses, and said solemnly, "Let me put it this way, Robyn. I'm an adolescent going through my phases."

That broke them up. They burst into laughter, and with that, the voices outside ceased. When the girls carried in the coffee and a plate of cookies, they were met by silence. They sat drinking coffee in silence. At last, Ethel said in a tight voice, "George wants you to remember, Robyn, that your real home is still here."

"Thanks. Is that the way you feel, too, Mom?"

"It depends."

"On the rules, Mom?"

"But *he* has his own home now, hasn't he? What does he want with you? Why does he get you and us involved this way?"

"That's not the way I see it, Mom. You forbade me . . ."

"He's working, isn't he?"

"Yes."

"And is he drinking, too, Robyn?"

George protested, "Now, Ethel . . ."

Ethel rushed on, "He can be dangerous when he drinks. That's all I'm trying to say, George."

"I'm sure Robyn's aware of that."

"Are you, Robyn? Are you? It's you I care about,

worry about. Won't you please stop being so stubborn? Robyn, I'm asking you to put a stop . . ."

"Oh, Mom . . . Mama!" Robyn cried. "It's no use, is it?" Even as the words burst from her, she felt she wanted to run to her mother, hold her, feel her mother's strong love flowing into her again. But her mother's voice was going on, piercing her feelings like a peevish child.

" . . . to the way he's victimizing you and this whole family. Just come home."

"And if I did that?" Robyn stammered.

"I've told you. Let the dead stay dead."

"Oh, Mama . . ."

The rapport, so tenuous from the start, was utterly destroyed, and Robyn felt, once more, that she had no choice. Suddenly very tired, she picked up her books.

"I guess I'd better go."

Ethel sat stiffly, refusing to meet Robyn's look. "All right. Just remember he can be dangerous when he's been drinking," she repeated tonelessly.

George saw Robyn to the door.

All the way back to the apartment, the sense of danger persisted, and now, at the late hour, the apartment was empty. She made herself a light supper of scrambled eggs and toast, and waited for Robert.

She stared miserably at the bottom bureau drawer, her mother's words affecting her with a strange insistence, then went to look.

A new bottle of gin lay there, like a living threat. She closed the drawer and felt as she always felt when she looked—somehow dirtied. She stacked the supper dishes in the sink and went to her room.

But she couldn't concentrate on her homework. The hour grew very late, and she listened to the radio, trying desperately to drown out her mother's warning. She stayed this way until the late news, and tried to focus on that for half an hour.

Why hadn't he phoned?

Where the hell was he?

The car wash closed at seven-thirty . . .

But not the bars.

I should have been here. Maybe he was worried about me.

Was he in some trouble?

Was he with that crazy Mimi?

Oh, God, why do I feel so scared?

At last, she went to bed, leaving her door slightly ajar. She was deep in some muddled dream about forest witches, and yellow scarfs hanging from branches, and aviator glasses as big as saucers, when human noises in the apartment woke her up. She made out her father's voice, trying to shush someone who was apparently bumping against the furniture. She heard Robert struggling to get the bottom drawer of the bureau open.

Robyn got up and put on her bathrobe. She stood in the doorway, and heard them stumbling around in the dark, and switched on the lights.

Her father had the stopper off the bottle, and a tall, stout, bosomy woman with stringy black hair falling into her eyes was saying, "Where the glasses, Bobby?"

Robert stared across the room at Robyn. His hands shook and his eyes were glazed. "That you, love? This . . . Mimi."

Mimi said, "Hi," and got two glasses out of the cupboard. She held them up. "Don't be stingy, Bobby. I gotta real thirst all over again." He poured the gin. The woman held her glass toward Robyn, giggled the way she did on the phone, and drank greedily.

Robert, holding on to the bottle, sat down heavily, swilled down the contents of his glass, and poured himself another.

Robyn said. "Daddy, get her out of here."

The woman had put down her glass, and now from her bag she drew out a piece of cigarette paper and a tiny box. Robyn had seen kids in the school lavatories roll marijuana the way the woman made her joint.

"Hey, Mimi." Robert mumbled, "don't light up in here. Whatcha doin' here, anyway?"

"I got you home, didn't I, honey?" the woman said, lighting up. "There's appreciation for you. Pour me another, Bobby." She took off her shabby corduroy jacket and slipped off her shoes, and now she sat down and passed the joint to Robert. He waved it back to her.

"If you don't get her out of here, Daddy . . ."

"What'll ye do?" the woman said. "Call the cops?"

"No, Daddy, *I'm* going to leave."

"Robyn girl, I'm sorry, I'm sorry." He stood up very shakily but, it seemed, nearly sobered by her words. "Now don't talk like that. I'll get her out."

"Right now."

"I don't feel so good, Bobby. Gotta stay here."

"You can't, baby. Robyn says you can't. Come on. Get your shoes on. Where're your damn shoes? Get you a taxi."

He tried to lead her to the door. When she resisted, he pushed her with his shoulder and got her there. Terribly shaken, Robyn handed the woman her jacket and shoes.

"How do I know she *is* your daughter? Hey?" the woman suddenly yelled. "Tell me that!"

"Keep your stupid voice down," Robyn said coldly.

She turned away from them in disgust and fear.

"Back in a jiffy, Robyn girl," she heard her father say as he made the woman put on her shoes, and got her out. She opened the window wide after they had gone, and could hear them, arguing and giggling, on their drunken way up the quiet street.

Then she took the bottle and poured the rest of the gin down the sink, and stood the empty bottle back on the table. Staring at it. Suddenly recalling the Puritan girl's line: "The parlor's packed with people, sir!"

21.

In the days that followed, her father, frightened and re-
pentant, stuck to his job at the car wash, and stayed away
from the bars and, apparently, Mimi. He told Robyn he
couldn't remember a thing about that night; he couldn't
imagine how he could have involved her with "that
tramp." But she also had to understand, he went on in a
pleading way, that it had been years since he'd been with
a woman, "and you're old enough for me to level with
you, Robyn girl."

"That's not the chief thing to worry about—my involvement," she replied sharply, trying to put down the
self-pitying note in his voice. "I'm worried about your parole rules. You're violating them, and that could be dangerous. What you did," she went on, her voice rising
roughly, "was crazy, wasn't it?" With a shock she became
aware that her voice sounded like her mother's—echoing
the same words which Ethel had been using, words of
fear and scorn. But it's all your fault, damn you, she
thought, putting me into such a stupid situation—your
own daughter. "The whole thing scared me," she said.

"Well, even my kind of P.O.," he muttered vaguely,
"knows it's natural to want a woman."

"A tramp on drugs?"

"She's not so bad," he protested. "And she got me
home, remember."

"She was looking to crash here, that's all!" Even as
Robyn said it, flat out, she wondered how much of his ra-
tionale was self-pity or self-hatred. The sense of danger
remained acute.

One afternoon she stopped her clerical work at the Center, and went to speak to Johnny. She didn't give him all the sordid details of the episode; but he seemed to guess them anyway.

"I'm so worried, Johnny," she said.

"You're right not to bottle it up. Robert's well aware of his own danger, you can be sure, the way he went berserk once and killed a man when he'd been drinking. I'm not a psychologist, but I know, from my own experiences, that one part of you will always keep on punishing yourself. Especially if you're basically a decent man, with decent ambitions in life. He can say all he likes that it couldn't happen again. It not only could, but, in a way, it already has, you know."

"That thing in his boss's office?" she stammered.

Johnny nodded coolly. "His P.O. learned about it, and he could have arrested Robert then. But the boss called me, and said he wasn't about to press charges because of a bottle of liquor being wasted. Even so, that P.O. is sure as hell storing up 'technicals' like that—and when he has enough, he can 'violate' your father pronto. Then it's back to the slammer for Robert."

"What can *I* do, Johnny?"

"You? Stop letting him use you, for one thing!" the big man exclaimed. Then he was cool again: "What I mean is that these ex-offenders *have* to ke responsibility for their actions, and not pull those they love down with them. If he ever hits the bottle again, I want you to leave him to go back down to the gutter alone. Now, I want your promise on that. because he could be dangerous again."

"I promise, Johnny."

"This place is open twenty-four hours, and you can come here and sleep overnight in the office, if you have to, until you either go home to your mother or find another place to live until you're off to college. Okay?"

"Okay. But he's so sorry, Johnny."

"Good. What he's got to do is to get sober and stay sober. For starters, he should be in A.A.—Alcoholics Anonymous—get to their meetings on a regular basis and accept their A.A. way of life which means a lot of self-understanding, and *never* another drink."

"He told me he was a member of A.A. in prison. That it's not his bag any more, and he knows how to stay sober."

"Does he now?" Johnny said grimly. "I'll just have to have a talk with your father."

Robert showed no resentment when she told him she'd spoken to Johnny and had set an appointment for the two men to talk. After the talk, Robert began to attend A.A. meetings near the Center. The bottle disappeared from the bureau drawer. When Mimi telephoned, he hung up on her and told Robyn to do the same thing. He began to favor tall glasses of tomato juice at dinner and bedtime. He got home after work, stayed in most evenings, seemed to be relieved that his life had some regularity.

He began to talk enthusiastically to Robyn about a new friend he'd made in Shaun, who also worked at the car wash. A former marine and machinist. Shaun, he said, was an ex-con like himself but younger, only twenty-four. He'd done time at Auburn State Prison for armed robbery, but his P.O. had taken a personal interest in him while he was still in prison. His P.O. had managed to bypass channels and help Shaun get paroled after he'd served three years of his six-year sentence and had helped Shaun get into a rehabilitation program in Manhattan. It was called the Fortune Society, and it helped ex-cons.

"Shaun swears by that P.O. He goes to him like he's his father, anyway, a real friend. He visits with him, gets his advice, has coffee with him. That man's *civilized*, Shaun says."

"That's nice for Shaun."

"I've been shortchanged with mine sure enough."

"Would they let you switch P.O.'s, Daddy?"

"You're joking! Ex-cons aren't in control of their supervision. You take what you get."

"What's to stop you from going with Shaun when he visits his P.O.?"

"Maybe you've got something there, baby."

And afterwards, he did go with Shaun once.

The sense of danger receded, but not for long. The bottle reappeared in the bureau. And the telephone calls from Mimi became more insistent. There were now times when Robyn got home from school or the Center when she could smell Mimi's cheap perfume in the apartment—or was it perfume?—and speculated that her father and the woman had used the apartment during her absence.

She remembered Johnny's admonition, and faced her father with it. "I've promised Johnny that I'll leave if you quit A.A. and go back to drinking." He pleaded that it wasn't the way she thought: "I have to feel a bit free, girl, after all those caged-up years. I'm in a rotten job, I can be laid off any time, I can't find myself at all, at all . . ."

"But you know what drinking can do to you?"

"Helps me to forget, Robyn girl."

"Isn't it better to remember, Daddy?"

"Remember? What?" he muttered, twisting away, and she was too tormented to remind him. But in her frustration, she managed to get out, "Johnny thinks you're using me. Are you using me?"

His faded blue eyes blinked in pain, and he asked, "Now how could I do that?"

"I suppose he means I make a good front for you, with your P.O. Something like that."

"Oh, child, is that what you think?"

"No, no."

"It's just . . . I'm frightened that the years are passing by and I haven't made anything of myself yet. Maybe I won't make it. That's what's bugging me, Robyn. I want to better myself for your sake."

"For your own sake, Daddy."

And they hugged each other close for a moment after that. Next day, when the telephone rang and it was Mimi, Robyn heard him say firmly he couldn't see her any more. No, he had no money to give her. He was making plans to go out of town to find a better job. And was that clear?

When he hung up, he said ironically, "She knows damn well I was lying. She's an ex-con herself, and she knows parolees aren't allowed to go out of town, or even out of neighborhoods without permission. And I'm as likely to get that from my P.O. as to get to the moon."

At any rate, the ambition to move on in terms of bettering himself persisted. He studied the want ads now, and had long talks with the administrators of the Fortune Society about going on with his education. The Society on East Twenty-second Street held weekly "rap" sessions, run by the ex-con staff members, to help parolees to readjust from institutional to street life; it was supported by the community and legislators and provided decent surroundings for ex-offenders to come and talk over their problems and get help with them.

The Fortune Society got out its own newspaper which went into prisons as well as legislative halls. The big framed slogan adorning its entrance was: TODAY IS THE FIRST DAY OF THE REST OF YOUR LIFE.

The Society sent him out on a couple of prospective jobs. So far they were only promises for the future. But he liked the way the Society accepted him, and everyone else who'd once collided with the law, as a human being and not as an ex-prison number, as someone who had potential for self-help. So he kept on with them, and he kept trying. Hard.

Then the world came crashing down on Robert Adam and his daughter.

It was the swift and mindless way in which it happened that stunned her. Later, trying to piece the reason for it together was like trying to catch a cloud.

It came without warning.

One evening she was going over her part in the play, and to her father's delight, she was giving him line readings while he held the script and filled in the other several parts himself. The shades were drawn, the apartment cozy, they had mugs of coffee at hand, and Robyn felt wonderfully animated showing off for her father.

She wore a peasant blouse over her jeans and the red

silk scarf on her shoulders, and had kicked off her shoes, and was executing a wild sort of dance to illustrate her number near the witch's brew in the forest, when a banging on the front door broke into the scene.

She stopped the dance, and her father went to answer the banging.

Mortimer Locke, his parole officer, was at the door. He pushed by her father without a word, and came and stood strangely. staring hard at Robyn. She was still breathless from the dance, her face flushed with exertion. Her hair hung in wild profusion. Now, under the P.O.'s gaze. Robyn felt a sudden terror. The animation in her face died, and she stammered out, "What are you doing here? Who let you in the building?"

22.

The P.O. looked every inch the bullyboy her father and Johnny had described. Bald-headed, muscular, business-suited, with one breast pocket neatly lined with ball-point pens, the jacket barely concealing a holstered gun on his hip pocket, the man dominated the room. Robyn fell back under his look, which seemed a curious mix of contempt and interest.

"Super let me in, of course. Who else?"

Robert asked testily, "Did you have to do that? Show him your badge? Burst in like . . . like gangbusters?"

"Yes."

"Why? All you had to do was ring my bell."

"Can't you guess why?"

"No."

"Well, for openers, you haven't kept your appointments with me."

"I did telephone you."

"I said appointments. Office. On time."

"I've had a few problems . . ."

"I'll say. Turn out those drawers."

"What?"

"The bureau, man. You going to turn them out or will I?"

"Sir, this is my daughter, and I'd prefer . . ."

"I know she's your daughter. We met."

"I'd prefer another time."

"*You'd* prefer. You forgetting the rules, man? Let me see, Parole Regulations, number four-a, I quote: 'I will permit my parole officer to visit me at my residence or place of employment.' "

Robyn stared at the man with fascination. He had reeled off the regulation as routinely as though he'd done it a thousand times before. He was going on, "And that means any time *I* choose to visit. What about the drawers."

Robert's thin face was white with desperation.

"You don't need her, Mr. Locke. Robyn, why don't you go to the Center, just till . . ."

"She stays. No one leaves until I've finished my search."

"Search for what?"

"We'll have to see, won't we?"

"But she's not involved in any way."

"Like hell she's not. She lives here, doesn't she?"

"She just . . . stays over now and then."

"Stop your lying, man."

Robyn put in very quietly, "It's all right, Daddy. We haven't done anything wrong." She went on more boldly, remembering the bottle in the bottom drawer, "You've made some mistakes in your own life, too, haven't you, sir?"

"I'll do the questions, miss," he replied. But he left off staring at her, and turned his full attention to Robert. She felt a deep loathing for the intruder, but seeing her father's desperation, she wanted above all to stay in control.

"Sit down," the P.O. ordered.

They complied, and now he strode around the small apartment, demonstrating who was master at that moment. His jacket flapped back now and then, clearly showing the presence of the gun, as he searched for something. If he knew what it was, he didn't let on immediately. He flung aside the cover of Robert's sofa-bed and looked behind and under the seat pillows. He shoved furniture around in his search. Deliberately ignoring the bureau as he knelt down, then straightened up, he went to Robyn's room and through her desk and ran his hands behind her books on the shelf.

All the while keeping them seated, silent and waiting until he could address himself to what he'd really come to search. Now he concentrated on the bureau, flinging out everything that the drawers contained, starting with the top drawer—Robert's shirts and socks and underwear; her underclothes and sweaters and panty hose and pajamas. All were flung about and at their feet as they sat immobilized in their horror. The P.O. was obviously trying to "psych" them into some sort of retaliation, and Robyn, watching her father's agonized face, kept her hand on his arm to restrain him.

Before the man got to the bottom drawer, Robyn said very distinctly, "You'll find some gin there. That what you came for?"

"That all?"

"What else, for God's sake?" Robert cried.

"This." He drew out from under the drawer's oilcloth lining a small glassine envelope, It contained several "roaches"—the butt ends of marijuana cigarettes.

"What are those?" Robyn stammered, as he held them up.

"Pot. Maybe other dope."

Her father's head went down in absolute shock. "Oh, Christ, that Mimi. She did it! She the one who put you up to this, Locke?"

The man took out the bottle of gin and put it on top of the bureau. He pocketed the glassine envelope with its contents.

"Let's go, you two," the man said.

"But why? They're not ours!" Robert cried.

"Of course not. Never are," the P.O. said dryly.

"Okay, so I had someone here. But no more. She doesn't come here any more. She must have left those behind. Be reasonable, man," he pleaded.

"Listen, I've been reasonable long enough. You don't report in, you attack your boss, you drink, you're on pot and now . . ."—his eyes were gazing again on the disheveled Robyn—"you're endangering the morals of this minor."

"That's not true!" Robyn cried. "Daddy's working, he's trying hard. I go to school and work, and I'm accepted for college. He was finished with that woman, and she's . . . she's framed him!"

"You've been watching too many TV crime stories," the man said. "Anyway, until we investigate this, you're *both* under arrest."

"She's not involved!" Robert shouted. He got to his feet, his eyes glittering with hatred. There was no drink in him now, and he stood, as rigid as steel, facing his tormentor. For a moment the P.O. seemed uncertain, and Robyn got up and clung to her father.

"Daddy, this can't be serious. It isn't fair. We haven't done anything, so let's go with him."

"No! You're not going anywhere!"

There was a terrible silence in the apartment. Then they saw the parole officer begin to reach for his gun. Robert said heavily, "Don't do that, Locke, I'm asking you not to show that in my home. She's not involved in any way, and you know it! You want to turn me in, okay, but leave her out of it!"

"And I'm saying that it's my job to take her in, too," the man said, but his hand, reaching for the gun, still hesitated. "I have no choice, Adam, since she's a minor. And I found the evidence in the bureau."

"And I say you're not going to arrest her."

In the next moment, she witnessed two terrifying things: the man almost had his gun out, and her father hit the man with an awful blow that bloodied Locke's right eye. Locke hit the floor. He tried to get up, but Robert was on top of him, hammering with his fists at the P.O., all the violence and hatred inside him being poured onto his target, until Locke lay unmoving under the assault. Trembling with fear and terror, Robyn at first was immobilized, staring helplessly from one to the other. Then she ran to her father, and tore at him, and screamed at him, "Stop it! You'll kill him!" When blindly he continued to pummel the man, she tore her father's arm back screaming into his face now, "You bastard! Are you crazy? Do you want to kill again then? *Well, do you*?"

Her father fell back. His faded blue eyes, hard and unseeing, stared into hers, and in that moment she suddenly felt she was looking into the face of a stranger. As she recoiled herself, she was aware of memory spinning backward in time. It was as though an old newsreel was being rerun: she was "seeing" how it had happened with Robert and Grandma's husband; how it *must* have happened then, six years ago, when her father was able to attack a man with such ferocity that the blows had killed.

She saw him stare like a blind man at the stricken P.O., then slowly get to his feet. His face was grey, and he nursed his knuckles; then as the blood flowed back into his cheeks and he seemed to be taking stock of his deed, he began berating himself.

"Oh, God, Robyn, what's the matter with me? I was only trying to protect you, and now look what I've done! Go to Johnny!" he was urging. "You can't stay around here. Tell Johnny to get me a lawyer. Go on, Robyn. Get going!"

Robyn got to her feet. The terror and shock still pounded at her temples. She pushed her father away. She felt confused, but she seemed to know instinctively what she must do. For one wild moment, she seemed to be standing outside her skin and was her mother, Ethel, spurred into doing what Ethel would do in this crisis. She realized, not without pain, that the fear she felt was more for the man than her father, as she ran to where the intruder had placed the bottle.

She poured some of the liquor into a small glass and got a pillow. Then she knelt down near the P.O. and put the pillow under his head, and forced some of the gin into his mouth. And she stayed with the man until he regained consciousness. Then she helped him to his feet. She stood to one side, white-faced and feeling drained.

Locke was shaky as he dusted himself off. He looked at Robyn curiously, and managed to murmur, "Thank you, miss."

To Robert, who stood near the door, watching the episode with all resistance obviously gone, Locke said, "It's a good thing she kept you from the gun. I mean, lucky for me, too. You realize you've just committed another major crime?" He slipped handcuffs on Robert, who was seemingly lost in some private nightmare.

"Let's go," the P.O. said to them.

23.

Robyn went with her father to the precinct house, Parole Officer Locke booked Robert for criminal assault. He watched his prisoner being fingerprinted, and gave his statement to a receiving officer. Locke now wore two hats, as it were: as P.O. and also as arresting officer. Robert, in addition to being a parole violator, would face new charges for his new offense, which was described as a "Grade A felony." A major new crime.

He was locked up overnight in the small detention pen; next morning he would be transported to the Manhattan Criminal Court for an "arraignment" where "reasonable cause" would have to be shown for holding him in prison pending a thorough investigation on charges.

Manhattan Criminal Court, where it all began, Robyn thought miserably. She looked at her father, now behind bars again. He was already a broken man.

"Take care of yourself, Robyn."

She went to where the P.O. was still dictating his statement to a clerk.

"Are you putting down," she asked very distinctly, "how you provoked and tried to humiliate my father in front of me? Are you putting all that in?"

The P.O. looked at Robyn thoughtfully. "I brought you here as a witness. We're not going to hold you. Do you want to give your own statement?"

"Do I have to now, without a lawyer?"

"No."

"Then I'm free to go?"

"Where can we reach you?"

"At my father's . . . at *our* apartment."

"Okay. Be in court tomorrow, ten o'clock, for your father's arraignment. Here's the address of Criminal Court. Know how to get there?"

He wrote it down, and when she saw it, the tears came at last as she turned away from the P.O.

"I know where it is," she said.

Johnny went with her next morning. He was careful in his attire for the court appearance, looking as dignified as a banker in his neat suit, striped tie, and polished shoes. He believed in the importance of making a good impression as a character witness, if called. He stood with Robyn inside the rail, in the well below the judge's bench. The court-appointed Legal Aid lawyer, provided for indigent prisoners, stood next to Robyn. A slight, bespectacled young man, recently out of law school, he had only a few minutes with Robert in the "holding pen" outside the courtroom, and brief minutes with Robyn and Johnny to clue himself in on the charges, before the black-robed judge took her seat.

She riffled through a thick file of papers, presumably the file on Robert Adam, as the prisoner was brought in by a uniformed officer of the court. Robyn, who had herself hardly slept all night, was shocked at her father's haggard appearance. He'd obviously slept in his clothes and hadn't shaved. His faded eyes stared ahead blankly, until they found Robyn; though they brightened then, they seemed to be the staring eyes of a blind man.

Then he was standing beside her, his tall, gaunt frame leaning forward toward the judge. The soft-spoken, greying woman could hardly be heard beyond her bench. She was saying that she'd read the arresting officer's statement, also the list of the prisoner's parole violations, and the fact that he was a repeater.

The word "repeater" made an indelible impression on Robyn, as she remembered how the scene of last night had gone back in memory . . .

The Legal Aid man was vigorously interposing that he

could establish intimidation and provocation of the prisoner; that the member of the family, present, saw it all; that he also had a character witness . . .

Robert said in a low voice, "Your Honor, my daughter shouldn't be here. She should be in school."

"Did she witness the assault?"

Robert mumbled his reply.

"Speak up, please."

"Yes, your Honor."

"Then it's all right for her to be here." She turned to Robyn. "Are you here for your father?"

"Oh, yes! He was—we were both—terribly upset by what Mr. Locke did."

"That will be investigated later, young lady, and all the facts gone into. Even so, there is a prima facie case here—that is, reasonable cause—to hold the prisoner, pending the investigation." She closed the manila folder, wrote something on its cover, and rubber-stamped it. "I'm setting a high bail on this case, because of this prisoner's previous record. Fifty thousand dollars." Robyn gasped.

The Legal Aid lawyer started to protest at the "unreasonably high bail . . . can't possible raise anything like that, your Honor . . . he's only out of prison a short time," but the soft-spoken judge cut him off.

"It's the nature of this assault," she said firmly. "He's killed a man already."

Johnny asked if he could speak, and the judge assented. His tone, respectful, was tinged with irony. "He killed in the Vietnam war, your Honor. Your file has that, too. I'm not defending his violence, but a lot of it may be traceable to those experiences. He won't get any help on that problem, you know, if he's behind bars."

"Now let's not intellectualize this alleged crime at this first hearing," the judge snapped, her patience suddenly at an end. "This prisoner is a repeater. My first duty is to protect society. The investigation will deal wih the facts and his background. Next case."

Robyn stayed on at the apartment. She went on with

school, rehearsals, the publication work, the Center, and talked about Robert's coming trial to no one. In this time, Robyn forced herself "to go through the motions," a term—and a frame of mind—that she had picked up at the Center, listening to Johnny's admonitions to new-comers. One "went through the motions"—of living, working, walking, sleeping, waiting for the healer, time it-self, to work its best at its own pace. So though she some-times felt at the point of emotional paralysis, she went through the motions and got on with her life.

But nothing in life had prepared her for this series of blows, and only some instinctive part of her mind kept reaching for self-control and kept her going. But going alone.

She did not try to visit George and Ethel again in this period; in fact whenever possible, she even avoided con-tact in school with Joyce. Though Joyce was one person whom she privately wished she could be with now. She was glad of the growing rapport between them, cherished it. Joyce would never be one of those who might say, "I told you so."

She could not avoid running into Victor in class, some-times in the library. But she found, to her vague surprise, that she really wanted to avoid him now. He definitely would be one of those mouthing that "I-told-you-so" cliché—probably not in so many words, but certainly by a look or a parental quotation. No, her spirit didn't need and more dampening just then. So she pressed on. In fact, she went through the motions so successfully at rehearsals that Carnovsky told her, with flourishes of her white or orange or mauve silk scarfs, that she was "Abby in the flesh."

She was touched, but not altogether pleased about that: Abby was a mean-spirited if beautiful creature and not at all grown up. But Robyn felt that she herself had not only grown up but was handling problems which would proba-bly defeat an older and wiser person. At least, she was trying to handle them.

Once, in the library, Shelley Clark crossed the room to

talk to her. Shelley's eyes were sparkling with good news: she had been accepted for the summer course at Cornell University before the formal opening in September. What about Robyn entering that course, too?

"I'll have to think about it," Robyn said.

The other looked so alive and happy that for a moment, Robyn yearned to tell her about her father. But the moment passed: she could not bring herself to tell Shelley, even with her own experiences, about the new disgrace to the family.

Robert had been removed to Rikers Island prison where it was difficult to visit him. The lawyer warned that parole investigations sometimes take months and months. She wrote Robert several times a week: by working at the Center she could keep the apartment, at least until she graduated. Then she would be going upstate to college, perhaps starting with the summer course. She missed him terribly, she wrote, and she was certain that in time, things would get better for him.

She was, of course, whistling in the dark, and she knew it. She felt that her near-solitary confinement seemed to be developing into some form of self-inflicted punishment. When she dreamed now, which was often, she seemed to be struggling through a dark tunnel. She couldn't find her way.

Then the ringing of the telephone, one evening shortly after Robert's imprisonment, seemed to promise one way into the light. A strange man on the phone was asking for her father.

"He's not here," she said, her guard up.

"Is this Robyn?"

"Well . . . yes, it is."

"Robyn, this is Shaun at the car wash. You've heard of me? I've been wondering what's happened to Robert. Has he quit or what?"

The man's words poured out, genuinely worried.

"Oh, Shaun, thank you for calling."

"Where's your dad then, Robyn?"

"He's in such trouble, Shaun!"

There was a pause. "I'm sorry. Can I help?"

"I hope so. Oh, yes, I hope so!"

"Want to meet me at Frank's place, for coffee?"

"Yes. Please!"

"I can be there in an hour."

"I'll be there, Shaun."

All she was really remembering, in that first moment of contact with Shaun, was that he had a parole officer whom he trusted and respected. And that her father had once visited with him. Maybe, she thought desperately, she could get help from the same quarter. Hadn't Shaun told her father that the P.O. had cut through some legal and bureaucratic red tape that had been snarling him, in prison and out?

Shaun was at Frank's before her—a slender, tense young man of medium height with a stock of red hair that was already streaked with gray. He listened very quietly to Robyn's story of the sadistic break-in and search by Robert's P.O., of her father's violent reaction to the humiliation, the "planted" evidence, the arrest, the imprisonment. Only once did he interrupt with a sad, small oath, when Robyn got to the assault part.

Shaun asked if she'd like to meet his P.O., and tell him the story, too. After all, his P.O. had met Robert once, and Robert had liked him. Maybe he knew some way to help . . .

"I was praying you'd say that," Robyn said. "Could you phone him now, Shaun?"

"What can we lose? I'll do it now."

When Shaun returned to their booth, he was all smiles. "He says he'll meet you here tomorrow, after school. Okay?"

"Daddy said you were his friend, Shaun."

24.

She got through the next day without feeling that she was "going through the motions." On the contrary, she felt fully aware of everything, and looking forward to the meeting with the new P.O.—one David Howard. She was told that he'd been a former assistant district attorney, who had switched careers to work as a parole officer inside the prison system, and now was doing his parole work on the outside. Lots of mixed experiences to count on there. So "hope" was the word for it as she prepared to meet him.

She went home first. She showered and changed from the worn blue jeans and denim shirt to her yellow sweater-and-skirt birthday outfit. She wanted to look her best, borrowing the idea from Johnny's example for his court appearance. Who could tell how the man might react to first contact? She donned very light makeup, and brushed her thick, auburn hair till it shone and fell straight and glossy over her shoulders. Then she tied the red silk scarf to her tote bag for luck.

This time she had to wait alone for a while in Frank's Coffee House, sitting in the booth near the door. So often had it become her meeting place that she had gone to it routinely. Olaf the Stick was on a bar stool, looking very skinny and wretched. He saw her come in, and seemed about to start toward her. But Robyn shook her head vigorously, and he stayed where he was. His head went down over his coffee cup. He seemed lost to the world.

Probably using drugs again, she thought, and her own head went down nervously. When she looked up again,

David Howard stood at the booth, smiling at her tentatively.

"Miss Adam? No, don't get up."

They shook hands. He slid into the seat opposite, dropping his bulging briefcase beside him. Then he sent her a look of such pure appreciation that she was thankful she looked her best.

"Shaun said to look for the prettiest female."

"You mean, the *only* female, don't you?" she murmured, and he grinned broadly. "Thank you for coming, Mr. Howard."

"That's okay. The name's David."

He loosened his sports jacket and tie, and motioned to the waitress. Robyn leaned back, studying him while he studied the menu.

She had been prepared for his ease of manner; Shaun had clued her in to his warmth and self-assurance. What she was not prepared for was the instant rapport which she felt with him. He was completely different from anyone she had ever known.

He was a tall man, but he didn't tower over one because of his slouchy manner. He might be any age, from early to late twenties. His slightly lined face had laughter wrinkles cut into the skin near his eyes and mouth. His coarse brown hair fell in tight ringlets on top and he had a surprisingly high forehead. The deep, brown eyes, under bushy eyebrows, were steady and thoughtful, until that grin lit them up. Big hands held the large menu card—and it was the firm, warm handshake from the first which had both encouraged and confused her. Was that just his practiced approach in getting a person's confidence? Or was she being unduly cynical, and he was, as Shaun said, the genuine thing—someone with "fellow-feeling"?

Certainly he seemed to be instantly at ease with everyone. Smiling amiably at the waitress, he was ordering a cheeseburger, heavy on the relish and pickles, and coffee. "Been out all day and forgot entirely to eat," he told Robyn. "Do you want a sandwich or something?" When she shook her head, he told the waitress to bring them two orders of chocolate ice cream anyway "and the hell with the calories," he added cheerfully.

Robyn said, "Like a father indulging his child?" And could have bitten off her words. This was no time for cynical cracks, no matter what. But Howard only looked at her thoughtfully, and said, "No, I like chocolate ice cream. Want me to cancel yours?"

"No," she said in a small voice.

He reached into his briefcase, and drew out a ruled legal pad and pen. "Want to start telling me about it?"

For nearly an hour, she talked and David Howard listened. One thing was real enough: he was that rare animal—a listener.

He took copious notes, asked few questions, and then only to encourage her to open up frankly, no holds barred. So she went back in time to her life as a child with Ethel and Robert; to his wartime service, and their holiday in Key West; to Grandma and her influence on the family; to his drinking problem and the way he handled his aggressions; to the divorce which traumatized him while he was behind bars; to her own confusion thereafter with Ethel's new marriage and dicta; to his fears of his P.O. Mortimer Locke; to the episodes leading up to the latest assault and arrest; to the emergence of the woman Mimi and Robert's frame-up.

Once or twice, David made her digress and talk about herself: about school and her friends there, the coming school play, her college plans, and Johnny's strong role in Robert's life. And as she talked, the feeling of powerlessness began to fall away. For probably the first time in her life, she felt some psychological release from the painful memories, because of the patient and compassionate man who was also, she told herself, an authority figure.

"So in fact, when Robert was sent up the first time," he said at last, "he was a first offender in the eyes of the law."

"What does that mean exactly?"

"No criminal record. And the crime of killing wasn't premeditated."

"There is this violence in him, though. He was so wor-

ried about involving me that he might have . . ." she
shuddered, " . . . gone for the gun."

"That's the point, the real responsibility on people like
me," David Howard said. "We have to help the ex-offend-
er to find other ways of handling their aggressions—instead of beating up on people."

"But he's not a criminal!" she cried. "He's not!"

"I don't think he is a criminal personality. He needs
help on his problems, but he won't get that behind bars.
And if he gets too bitter, he could turn . . . criminal."

"That's what Johnny says," she said sadly.

He ordered another round of coffee when she finished and
he put away his notes. Then it was his turn:

"There are some things I want to look into with your
father's case. Ordinarily, I would hesitate to go to another
parole officer's supervisor about complaints. But as it happens, there have already been rumors about Locke's, uh,
techniques as I go about in the field, so your story will
just be one more. As my supervisor puts it, they know
there are some bad apples in this parole barrel, perhaps
not more than ten percent of the lot, and it's possible
. . ."—his eyelids drooped over his thoughtful eyes—
"that this particular P.O. has power which he can't control."

"What happens to the ten percent?"

"They get found out—and fired."

They drank their coffee and pondered that.

"Meantime, what's going to happen to Daddy?"

He looked at Robyn keenly, and when he answered
her, it was in a very quiet, precise tone, explaining the
law.

"Your father is guilty now of a new crime, Robyn—
criminal assault as well as parole violation. Moreover. the
assault was on his parole officer, than which," he added
dryly, "nothing is worse. Ex-offenders go back into the
slammer for that act alone. This P.O. apparently stored
up a few other 'technicals'—parole violations—against
Robert before the assault. You know about some of

those. And finally, he's a 'repeater' of the same sort of aggressive assault which landed him in prison in the first place. So he's being held until the investigation leading up to and including the new assault is completed. That's the first stage."

"But it's not fair!" she protested. "Tell me, if Daddy had the money for bail, would he even be held?"

"So we're not discussing what's fair in your terms just now. That particular judge wanted to make sure that *this repeater*,"—and David Howard sounded as solemn as the judge,—"was held, away from society, until his next court appearance."

"And when will that be?"

"That may take weeks, maybe months."

She felt so forlorn then that she could think of nothing to say except, bitterly, "But plenty of men get into fights and don't land in prison, don't they?"

"Don't be dumb, Robyn," the man said sharply. "You know this is different."

"I know. I'm sorry." And she felt very small and drained as she asked, "What happens to him now?"

"He's being held in Rikers Island prison, and if he's found guilty, he'll be transferred from there to a prison, a State facility, since he's also in violation of his parole. Quite possibly," he said carefully, watching Robyn's face go pale, "back to his former prison, Green Haven. What your father has done is called a Class A felony. If he comes before a tough judge, the sentence could be double what he was given before, up to ten-to-twenty years. If he comes before a compassionate judge, who's persuaded that there was provocation, the judge could dismiss the charge; nevertheless Robert still would be a parole violator and held for sentencing.

"At that point, if the charge is dismissed, the Parole Board would take over: This stage involves a lot of investigative work, taking an immense amount of time, to get to the bottom of such incidents as provocation and assault. We would have to investigate thoroughly just what sort of P.O. this man is, as well as what sort of prisoner

Robert Adam is. And rest assured of one thing," he continued grimly. "If any part of the provocation or piling up of 'technicals' for sadistic reasons is evidenced, I know that our Area Director would permanently fire that particular P.O. End his career of power over men."

"These investigations . . . they take a long time?" she stammered.

"Could be months."

"But why? They've got Daddy serving time before he's even been found guilty!"

She felt his gaze on her was not without pity. But his words came again with professional detachment. "Remember that Locke, the P.O., will be in there fighting for his rights and his job, and denying that he gave any provocation, and so on. Investigations like these have to be fair, with both sides heard, and that takes a lot of time."

"And you're saying that Daddy may be thrown back in that Green Haven prison?" she cried.

"Before this is all over . . . perhaps."

"Oh, my God!"

They fell silent. She held in her terrible fears. Why hadn't Daddy been lucky enough to have drawn a P.O. like you? she wondered. Then, yielding to her despair, she thought: If they get Daddy behind bars again, for months or years, how can he ever get help on his deep psychological problems there? All the experts, including this man, tell me that prisons don't rehabilitate—rarely change a person for the better—because the staff people inside can reach so few inmates; it's like putting Band-Aids on deep spiritual and psychological wounds. So why con the public into believing that prisoners were not only there for punishment, but also for their rehabilitation? What a fraud! How many others, like her father, leave the Wall, frightened and alone and jobless, with all the neurotic feelings and self-hatreds and aggressions still boiling up in them? Fearful, too, that for minor parole infractions, they'd be landing back behind the Wall again—repeaters, with sentences piled on top of their old sentences! When would an ex-convict ever feel free to be a *person* again?

"Does anyone really care about ex-convicts?" she wondered aloud, very weary now.

"I care!" David Howard shot back, with something almost like anger in his eyes. She was aware that the tight ringlets on top of his head were wet with perspiration, as though he'd been running the same race with emotions as she had. "I care a lot! A convict is first, last, and always a human being to me! More—he's a human challenge! Listen: people can talk about putting away the 'dangerous' prisoner. But we in the field know that there's no way to predict dangerousness. All scientists agree on that. The guy in for auto theft or simple burglary may seem like a minor criminal and passive; but he may be a fuse, a time bomb, waiting to go off when he comes out. The man may be potentially more dangerous than the armed robber, or the man who has killed in a passion. All the good parole officers can do is 'run interference.' "

"Meaning?"

"Meaning, he doesn't store up the infractions; he works to keep the prison off an ex-con's back. He gets the prisoner's confidence, so he can help the man to change. Just remember," he went on, "that for every P.O. who takes the cynical attitude that here's an ex-con who's going to 'fall' again, it's just a matter of time, there are those of us who feel—here's a man who's got problems, and how can I catch him and turn him around before he 'falls.' Now, drink your coffee."

She did as she was told.

She felt the pain inside her head begin to subside as she contemplated her new friend.

She asked, very quietly, "Do you think you can help my father to understand his problems, and to change?"

"I can try. If I can only get to him, early enough, next time he comes out."

Howard was leaning toward her. She was aware that the dark, brooding eyes reflected a sudden perplexity as he studied her face, and she felt herself flush as she returned his thoughtful look. An inner excitement stirred her in the moment's intimacy. He seemed to sense her own response, as he took her hand.

Then his easy grin came, wrinkling the skin near his eyes, and he drew back as he asked, "You're going to be all right, Robyn?"

She took a deep breath. "I feel I've been sleepwalking for days, but I've just woken up. I'm . . . very all right now."

"Good."

He drove her home, dropping her off at her father's apartment, saying he still had some field work to do. He gave her his office and home numbers, told her they'd meet again soon. "I'll move this investigation all I can."

As he drove away, he called out, "Stay strong."

Like an echo of Joyce. Well, much more than that.

She went in, feeling that at last she and Robert had someone on their side—someone with power to act.

25.

It was Joyce who told her it had been reported in the newspaper. They met at Joyce's beckoning in a far corner of the library, and she showed Robyn the *Daily News* clipping which described how "a parolee, Robert Adam, had assaulted his parole officer, knocking him unconscious, and was being held on Rikers Island for investigation." Robyn had stayed away from the papers for days, fearing what might be there; she was relieved, at least, to learn that the story was too unimportant to warrant more than a paragraph on a back page, near the crossword puzzle.

Robyn asked, "Did Mom see it?"

"Yes. George wanted to phone you, but Ethel said no, she didn't want us involved."

"How do you feel, Joyce?"

"Feel? I'm here, aren't I. dumb-dumb!"

Robyn sent her a fleeting smile. "Listen, do me a favor, *dumb-dumb*," she said suddenly. "Take those damn glasses off in my presence." Joyce's mouth dropped, but she took the glasses off and put them down on top of the clipping, and Robyn then leaned over and kissed her.

"Aren't we the sloppy ones?" Joyce cracked, but she was pleased. "Has it been hell, Robyn?"

"It's not been too gorgeous. But I'm learning."

"Want to talk?"

"Some time. I mean that."

"Thanks," said Joyce, picking up her glasses.

"Listen, you . . . keep those off!" Robyn said impulsively. "You've got such beautiful eyes, don't you know

169

that? And after you lose twenty-five pounds, you're going to be the best-looking junior in the whole school!"

"That all I have to do?" Joyce said, so solemnly that they laughed. But when she left. she was twirling the glasses between her thumb and forefinger.

"Mom, I have to see you."

"Oh, so you finally decided to phone."

"You know what happened, Mom."

"Of course."

"So I thought . . ."

"Now are you coming home, Robyn?"

"Coming home?"

"Well, that's what you want now, isn't it?"

"That's not the reason I'm calling you, Mom."

"Oh?"

"Mom . . . I love you, and I need to talk to you!"

"Well, don't say I didn't warn you . . . I told you . . ."

"Mom, will you listen to me, please?"

"Are you coming home or not, Robyn?"

"No . . . no, I don't think so, Mom."

"Then what's the use . . . ?"

"I told you. I need to talk to you, Mom."

"Well . . . all right, Robyn. I'll arrange to come home for lunch tomorrow. We can have the place to ourselves."

"That's fine."

"But be on time. I have to get back to work, you know."

"Thanks a lot, Mom."

"And Robyn . . ."

"Yes, Mom?"

"You know I love you, too."

"Oh, Mom, I've wanted to hear it."

"But dammit, you've been so crazy and strange, yes, and inconsiderate and selfish, too!"

"Mom . . . please!"

"Well, it's true. Well . . . see you tomorrow."

"Tomorrow. Thanks again, Mom."

As Robyn stood inside the Grenshaw apartment again, the sweet familiarity of the old-fashioned place, the stately piano with its sheet music spread on the piano stand, the blossoming plants at the bay window, even the big, empty-faced television visible in the living room seemed all to be drawing her powerfully back into the orderly orbit of her mother's life. She stood silently a moment, drinking in the serenity, gazing across at her mother who was waiting for her near the big overstuffed chair, "her chair."

In her neat, blue knit suit, the well-brushed blond hair framing her still youthful face, Ethel looked so pretty and small and vulnerable that Robyn ran to her. She threw her arms around her and kissed her fiercely. And Ethel held her close. She kissed the tears on Robyn's face, as she had when Robyn was a child, and they stood together that way for a long moment.

"We've had a bad time, Mom," Robyn said as they parted at last.

"That we have. But it's over now, isn't it? It's over and done with forever?" Robyn felt her mother's eyes, still wet with tears, searching hers for agreement. "I mean, you can wipe the slate clean and come home, can't you, Robyn?"

"We have to talk, Mom," Robyn replied, aware that her guarded tone was hurting the other. Her mother said querulously, "But what else is there to talk about?"

"So much, Mom."

"Well . . . all right. I've fixed some sandwiches and milk and coffee."

"Just some coffee, please."

They sat at the highly polished dining room table, with its centerpiece of pink tea roses, the lunch plates and silver arranged on circular place mats. Robyn felt it had all been prepared with care. It was so nostalgic: To ease the way back into the old life here? Rub out the past, especially the recent past . . . ?

She struggled with her emotions, as her mother waited

in silence for Robyn to take the initiative. Robyn could not help but wonder where to begin. So much had happened between them, to herself.

How can I rub out the past, Mom?

It's *there*, Mom!

Daddy's part of me, of my life.

And can't you see I'm not the same Robyn who left here?

But there's so much of you in me, Mom, and I had to talk to you about that.

I wanted to share that with you.

I'm not fantasizing. It's true.

I need to share it with you.

Like when I was a kid!

But I'm not a kid any more!

Her mother had broken the silence, and was saying in a firm tone, "I told you it could be dangerous for you, Robyn. You can't say I didn't warn you."

"You did, Mom."

"Well, was I right?"

"Yes. In a way."

"What way?"

"When Daddy beat up on his parole officer, that was the worst. I was so scared. I wanted to run."

"Why didn't you?" her mother asked in a horrified voice.

"I couldn't. Anyway, I was about to be booked, too, Mom, along with Daddy."

"Oh, good God!"

"But Daddy was changing, Mom. You must believe that. He was trying . . . really trying."

"And you, of course," her mother said, quite coldly now, "you were stage-managing that great miracle."

"Stop it, Mom! Don't start that again!"

Robyn saw her mother's eyes widen to circles of fear, and impulsively she reached to take her mother's hand, but Ethel drew back. "You never used to talk to me like that, Robyn."

"I'm sorry, Mom."

"Don't you know you brought all this on yourself?"

"So you keep saying, Mom." Robyn's voice hardened as she struggled to hold in her anger. "Well, I've got news for you, Mom. I'm not sorry I brought it 'on myself,' as you put it. I've learned a lot about myself these past months, about you, too, Mom, and Daddy. I know I've changed a lot."

"And *I* know I don't like what I see in you, Robyn."

Robyn stood up. "You should, Mom," she burst out passionately. "After all, there's a lot of you in me—including, thank God, some of your best instincts. Don't you know that?"

"What are you talking about?"

"I'm not sure I know. But there were times when I felt I was doing exactly what you'd be doing in my place."

Her mother stared at her.

"I'm sure you must think me very drab and dull," her mother began again, her voice rising accusingly, "after running off and living with . . . with him; and no doubt seeing his women and his drinking. And romancing about it all."

"Oh, Mama, it's not what you think!"

"You don't think I remember what it was like!" she rushed on bitterly. Robyn gazed at her mother in confusion, but she was vaguely aware of a curious quality in her mother's bitter attack. She hesitated before she managed to say, "You still do care about him, don't you, Mom?"

Her mother twisted away.

"I've never denied that I loved him. There was a time when it was . . . quite marvelous. But I've told you, over and over, he has ceased to exist in my life. And I had hoped, Robyn, in yours, too."

Robyn shook her head. "I know now, Mom, that I'll never give up on my father. You did. I won't. Because he's not a real criminal. He's made a lot of mistakes, and he's hurt people—and himself—and that's bad. And I'm not fantasizing any more, you know, about being his strong right arm or something. I know he needs a lot of help, not only from me when he comes out again, but professional help from . . . good people specially trained in helping ex-convicts." She swallowed hard and kept control as she continued, "Most of all from experts who are trained, as a friend told me, to reach out to men like Daddy before they 'take a fall.' "

" 'Take a fall'?"

"It's just a figure of speech, to describe people who feel so beaten by life that they do things they know will land them back in prison. Mom, what I said before when I said there's a lot of you in me, I meant that. I know you don't understand why I had to help Daddy—or you *won't* understand—but don't forget how you always protected me. You shouldn't be so surprised and angry then, because I've learned from you to love someone in the same way. Protectively."

They fell silent. The lowered venetian blinds shut out the noonday sunshine, so as not to fade the upholstery, but one ray had escaped the slats and fallen on the roses. Robyn saw her mother's gaze go from the flowers to the blinds, as though contemplating whether to draw them tighter. Then her mother shrugged, and got up and began to clear away the lunch dishes.

"There's one thing more I need to tell you, Mom. It's not easy." Ethel went on with her task, but she was listening. "When Daddy began beating up on his parole officer, and the man passed out on the floor, I was terribly scared, as I said, but I did something you would expect me to do, Mom. Something you would have done. Instinctively. I helped the man. Even though he'd behaved like a rotten, horrible pig to us, I helped him. *You* were there with me, Mom telling me what to do!"

Robyn watched her mother's face, and her throat felt tight.

Ethel hesitated. She looked at the bold ray of sunlight touching the table, as though it might be holding some kind of symbolism for her. Then she looked at Robyn, who waited for a sign that her mother understood how much they meant to each other.

When it came, the sting was out of her voice, and she sent Robyn a rueful smile.

"Well, I guess you're right about one thing, Robyn. You've grown up. Fast."

26.

———◆———

Robyn had saved enough money which, together with a scholarship award, would enable her to enroll in the summer course with Shelley Clark. If there was one thing above all that she wanted, she told herself, it was achievable goals to concentrate on during the coming months.

David had said that if the "provocation" were established, the charges against her father would probably be reduced considerably; in fact, countercharges would in that event be brought against the P.O. Locke who would himself have to stand trial by the Parole Board. So she kept the apartment for the time being, in hopes that her father, should he be released early enough, would have a decent and familiar home to come back to.

She had met with David several times since Frank's place, and once he let her go with him on his field work. He checked a few parolees at their places of business—by prearranging with each to come out to his old Chevy for brief chats, asking them to telephone him later. In this way, not one of the parolees' fellow workers knew about the P.O.'s appearances.

David's technique was, as Shaun liked to put it, "civilized. That's why we respect and trust him."

And one day he drove her to Rikers Island, so that she could visit Robert for a few hours, and reassure him that the investigation was really moving.

Afterwards, David drove her to dinner in a quiet place in Greenwich Village. It was well before the dinner hour and they had the small restaurant almost to themselves, and over glasses of white wine they talked and watched the human parade pass by the street windows. Mostly, they talked about themselves, and David's work, and her part in the coming play. He promised to come to the production.

What remained unresolved in that complex time were her relationships with those who, until recently, had meant everything in life to her: with Ethel, George, Joyce—and with Victor Burnside.

At least I feel a self-respect for what I did, Mom. I had to choose, and I chose the road I *had* to go.

David understands why I had to choose that road. I was at least trying to reach someone I loved before he fell.

I lost . . . I couldn't keep Daddy from falling this time.

But I intend to try again.

Because I have to.

Because I believe that's the right road to take.

I know now some of the fires you went through, Mama—but the difference between you and me is that I didn't stop loving him. He's part of me. I'm Adam's daughter.

I love him, and David says it's healthy not only to feel that but also to act on it.

Love *has* to be an active thing, he says.

When Daddy comes out, I won't be the only one he can turn to, because of David. We'll try to be there to catch him before he falls . . . But perhaps he won't fall. Perhaps he'll make it on his own. I have to believe that. I'm not his namesake for nothing.

The inner courtyard, that evening in May, seemed like a celebrant itself.

The mimosa tree was a sunburst of tiny blossoms, and a light breeze was blowing the yellow flowers of the forsythia bushes on the sculptures and stony walks. The amphitheatre was strung with Japanese lanterns and colored electric lights, lending enchantment to the scene. Several hundred students, relatives, and community leaders who had contributed their time and costumes and scenery to the play milled around before finding seats. A spotlight danced across the stage, and came to rest on Miss Carnovsky. She held up her hands, one of which held a broad swathe of orange satin, for quiet, and her welcome.

She fluttered the scarf and got attention, and expressed the school's gratitude to the community "for its support of great plays" (burst of applause) and "our great actors" (wild burst of applause) who were all going on to college having "survived the crucible of their tyrannical teachers" (laughter and whistles on that one).

Robyn stood in the wings, while Carnovsky did her turn, looking out at the audience. The lights were still up; and though she was already "Abby," the Puritan girl in pale blue cotton dress, pinafore and cap, she was very much herself as, with her fellow actors, she picked out her relatives and friends. Joyce was in the front row with Shelley Clark. A few rows behind them were Ethel and George, her mother looking very trim and youthful in a new brown suit and white gloves.

Plainly on view was Victor, leaning against a tree, with a group of his football friends. He wore his white fisherman sweater, and seemed very silent and apart in that small gathering.

Johnny had come, bulking large, like a weathered monument, near enough in the setting to her parents and Victor, but seemingly light years away from them. He spotted her looking out from the wings, and flashed her his big smile and handwave. Would Daddy ever be able to learn Johnny's secret of survival on the outside?

The one she anxiously hoped would come didn't seem to be there. Whimsically, David had sent her a good-luck card clipped to a bag of popcorn, which, he wrote, they'd share after the show—if he could make it. As she looked out, she tried to put down the awful feeling of fright before going on stage, and the added anxiety that perhaps he couldn't come.

She was still searching for him when Carnovsky, with a final flourish of the orange satin, finished, and came off, and the lights began to dim.

Then she saw David come in through the French doors and find a seat on the aisle. His jacket and tie were askew, as though he'd been hurrying. And though the stage fright persisted, another emotion, far less painful, now coursed through her, knowing that her friend was out there.

Carnovsky, eyes sparkling with excitement, had clearly loved her little turn on stage. She whispered to the first group who opened the show, "Go!"

The actors ran up the stone steps and took their places.

"Now you, Robyn! You're on!"

Then she was on. Fusing her life, for a brief moment, with that of the reckless Puritan girl in the strange drama of the past. But feeling also a strong, complex flow of spirit—of sadness mixed surprisingly with joy, and with wonder, too, about the new chapter in her own life, just beginning.

About the Author

Gertrude Samuels was born in England and went to school there, but later attended George Washington University in Washington, D.C. She was a staff writer and photographer for *The New York Times* for more than twenty-five years. She has contributed to many magazines including *The Saturday Evening Post* and *The Saturday Review* and is the author of a number of books including B-G: FIGHTER OF GOLIATHS, the story of Ben-Gurion; THE SECRET OF GONEN, the story of a border kibbutz; THE PEOP' E VS. BABY; and the bestselling novel, RUN, SHELLEY, RUN!

Young Adult Titles from SIGNET

☐ **DELPHA GREEN AND COMPANY** by Vera and Bill Cleaver.
(#Y6907—$1.25)

☐ **ELLEN GRAE AND LADY ELLEN GRAE** by Vera and Bill Cleaver
(#W8689—$1.50)

☐ **GROVER** by Vera and Bill Cleaver. (#Y6714—$1.25)

☐ **I WOULD RATHER BE A TURNIP** by Vera and Bill Cleaver.
(#Y7034—$1.25)

☐ **ME TOO** by Vera and Bill Cleaver. (#Y6519—$1.25)

☐ **THE MOCK REVOLT** by Vera and Bill Cleaver.
(#Y7502—$1.25)

☐ **WHERE THE LILIES BLOOM** by Vera and Bill Cleaver.
(#W8065—$1.50)

☐ **THE WHYS AND WHEREFORES OF LITTABELLE LEE** by Vera and Bill Cleaver. (#Y7225—$1.25)

☐ **I THINK THIS IS WHERE I CAME IN** by Phyllis Anderson Wood. (#Y7753—$1.25)

☐ **I'VE MISSED A SUNSET OR THREE** by Phyllis Anderson Wood. (#Y7944—$1.25)

☐ **SONG OF THE SHAGGY CANARY** by Phyllis Anderson Wood.
(#Y7859—$1.25)

☐ **WIN ME AND YOU LOSE** by Phyllis Anderson Wood.
(#Y8028—$1.25)

☐ **YOUR BIRD IS HERE, TOM THOMPSON** by Phyllis Anderson Wood. (#Y8192—$1.25)

☐ **NAVAJO SLAVE** by Lynn Gessner. (#W8128—$1.50)

☐ **NOTHING EVER HAPPENS HERE** by Carol Beach York.
(#Y7991—$1.25)

☐ **MR. AND MRS. BO JO JONES** by Ann Head. (#W7869—$1.50)

☐ **THE STORY OF SANDY** by Susan Stanhope Wexler.
(#W8102—$1.50)

☐ **JUST WE THREE** by Charlotte Herman. (#Q6758—95¢)

Buy them at your local

bookstore or use coupon on

next page for ordering.